ACE CARROWAY
AND THE
GHOST LINER

GUY WORTHEY

ACE CARROWAY AND THE GHOST LINER

This is a work of fiction. Names, characters, places, and incidents are either the product of the author's imagination or are used fictitiously. Any resemblance to actual persons, living or dead, is entirely coincidental.

Cover design: Guy Worthey

ISBN: 1-949827-00-3
ISBN-13: 978-1-949827-00-2

 Westing Press

In memory of Grandma Marie,

pioneer, flapper, schoolmarm, and lover of life.

THE ALASKA DAILY EMPI

"ALL THE NEWS 'ALL THE TIME"

VOL. XX., NO. 3072. JUNEAU, ALASKA, SATURDAY, OCTOBER 21, 1922. MEMBER OF ASSOCIATED PR

S. S. Jefferson Drops Propeller in Dixon E

S. S. JEFFERSON HAS ACCIDENT ON WAY SOUTH

Alaska Steamer Drops Propeller in Dixon Entrance —Aid Is Summoned.

The steamer Jefferson, of the Alaska Steamship Company, in command of Captain Livingston, dropped her propeller early last night while crossing Dixon Entrance southbound for Seattle from Southeastern Alaskan ports.

Wireless calls for aid were immediately sent out.

The lighthouse tender Cedar and Coast Guard Ship Smith, both at Ketchikan, immediately left for the scene.

According to wireless reports the two ships made good time, picked up the steamer Jefferson and after tow of the Cedar, escorted by the Smith, arrived at Ketchikan this morning.

According to cable advices received from the Ketchikan Chronicle no hardship was endured. The Jefferson will probably re-

Sues General's Kin for a Divorce.

[Mrs'Grace Fream'Ace-...
...sues Grace Fream, known as the Lady ou Grey Russell, has asked a divorce in Chicago from...

MISSING PERSON IN JUNEAU

JUNEAU, Oct. 21.—Morgan Mining executives informed the sheriff of a missing man yesterday. The man is Robert Bostock, a buyer for Cecilia "Ace" Carroway, Great War invalid and post-war shipping magnate. Her buyer arrived in Juneau early Thursday, but has not been seen since. A description is not available.

Alaska Steamship Company Awards Contract to Tacoma Firm for $1,000,000.

SEATTLE, Oct. 21.—Announcement was made today by the officials of the Alaska Steamship Company of the letting of a contract to the Todd Drydock & Construction Corporation of Tacoma for the construction of a $1,000,000 passenger liner for the Alaska route.

The vessel will carry 225 passengers and will have a speed of 15 knots an hour.

The steamer will have twin screws, and will be 365 feet in length, 48 feet beam and 28 feet depth of hold.

The liner will be completed for operation early next spring.

Gold Dust Reaches South

WOMEN'S DELEGATES TO SELECT 12 GREATEST AMERICAN WOMEN.

Mrs. Samuel McChintock, Miss Marion Parkhurst, Miss Lida Halford, Mrs. Maud W. Parks, Miss Mary Stuart & Mrs A. C. Watkins.

The women shown in this photograph have been chosen to select the twelve greatest living American women, asked for by Senorita Manejana, noted authoress, who wished to write about them for her Chilean papers. From left to right they are: Mrs. Samuel McChintock, of the Y. W. C. A.; Miss Marion Parkhurst, secretary of the National League of Women Voters; Miss Mary Stuart, of the Federation of Business and Professional Clubs, and Mrs. Arthur C. Watkins, of the Mothers' Congress and Parent-Teachers' Association.

M'ADOO SAYS VETS SHOULD

Offer to Exchange Living for Dead Is Turned Down

MANY ISSUES ARE INVOLVED

CHAPTER 1

In the tiny cabin belowdecks, the electric lights flickered and died. The deep throb of the steamer's engines ceased vibrating the iron walls. The poker game plunged into darkness.

"Oh, not again," said the Irishman, Gallows. His blunt face and rangy frame disappeared from view as the lights failed.

"A pity. My cards were good," said the Bostonian, known aboard ship as Bert. His full name, Hubert Ewing Devery Christopher Bostock III, was baggage too weighty for a few-day voyage.

Gallows chuckled in the dark. "Liar. 'Tis a lucky escape for you, Bert."

"Thanks for the game, Gallows."

"You're welcome, but 'twasn't much of a game. You and your five-penny limit. You and Brown both. I might as well whittle wood for all the profit I made. Good night. I'm off to my bunk."

"I think I'll go on deck. I hope the engineer beats his average getting the engines going. What is this, the fourth time? We're already a day and a half behind."

"He won't, but there's no use in worrying over it," the Irishman advised cheerfully. Gallows quit the tiny cabin.

Groping in the pitch black, the young Boston lawyer felt for the doorway. Once in the passageway, Bert shuffled until his toes bumped the stairs up to the deck of the little steamer.

The clammy chill of the night air slapped Bert like a soggy rag. He jammed his hands in his jacket pockets and hunched his shoulders. Presumably, somewhere in the bowels of the steamer, the captain and engineer cursed at machinery and sweated in the engine room heat. Bert's errand to purchase metal in Juneau must wait for them. On deck, Bert heard only the gentle plops of glassy waves against the hull. Even the persistent, raucous seabirds had vanished. Sleeping, no doubt. Now infinitely far from the wood-paneled courtrooms of Boston, the young attorney beheld a different world.

A gibbous moon wanly lit the ship and placid waters. The luminance waxed and waned as ponderous banks of fog slowly boiled. Bert shuffled to the prow of the becalmed vessel. The silvery landscape of mists formed insubstantial mountains of vapor over the gleaming waters of the inland passage. He searched in vain for the ragged dark lines of tree-covered shores. The entire world was composed of water, air, and uneasy mixtures of the two.

He shivered. The lone man's exhaled breaths exploded into tiny plumes of mist the moment they touched the cold, moist night. A desire for warmth overcame his appreciation of moonlight and sculptures carved of mist.

But before he turned his back on the scene, movement caught his eye. He stared forward.

An ominous darkness materialized from ahead. A vague towering mass moved inexorably toward him. Bert gripped the railing in alarm. His heart raced. Were they about to collide with a rock? But, no. That made no sense. They were stopped dead in the water.

The dark mass resolved into the flared shape of an elegant ship's prow. At first on a collision course, by degrees the oncoming vessel veered starboard, cutting through the mists. Moonlight patterned its dark outline, and portholes glowed with a greenish hue the color of bloodless skin. The evolving scene captivated Bert's round eyes.

Besides soft slaps of watery ripples, a series of clicks like a rusty door hinge stiffened his shoulders. The percussive background seemed to rise from the waters themselves. The ship cruised in a ghostly cocoon of fog and an eerie envelope of sonic accompaniment.

It was a luxury liner, crafted of steel and brass and panels of rich wood. The portholes offered glimpses of carved wooden chair backs and silver candlesticks on cloth-covered tables. No hint of smoke rose from its stacks, and yet the ship sailed. Its chill splendor paraded before the lone, slack-jawed watcher.

Standing in its prow much like Bert stood in the steamer's was a figure Bert at first took for a statue. But although the bearded apparition did not move, its wild hair glowed with moonlight or some internal radiance. It wore a captain's coat and a fisherman's cap, too realistic to be made of stone or wood. Twin points of greenish light gleamed beneath shaggy brows. The man, or ghost, stood upon one leg and one shaft of wood. Bert's throat constricted.

The ghost liner moved past. As silently as it arrived, it faded into the next fogbank. It dimmed to an indistinct shadow, and then it was gone.

Bert stayed on deck for two hours more, peering fruitlessly into the fog. He retreated to his bunk only when his teeth began to chatter audibly and uncontrollably. After he buried himself under a blanket, he muttered, "I can hardly believe my own eyes. I bet even Ace would be stumped."

The dark-haired lawyer rose late to find the steamer chugging away up the inside passage under a sparkling sun. No trace of the night mists could be seen, and tree-covered shores flanked the watery way. Bert had missed breakfast. By the time he persuaded the sluggish steward to toss him a biscuit, Juneau's harbor could be seen in the distance. Their destination, at last.

Bert packed his kit. He wanted someone to talk to, but none of the three crew members appreciated chit-chat. His fellow passengers, Brown, Gallows, and that Midwesterner were out of sight. Bert leaned on the rail and watched Juneau grow large.

"I need a drink," Bert muttered.

A bright voice boomed in his ear. "A drink? A drink?"

"Gallows! You startled me."

"What could I do?" Gallows's cheeky grin was positively infectious. "You mentioned drink. Music to an Irishman's ears. I happen to know of a pub. Several, really, but one in particular. Since you insist, I'll allow you to buy me a drink."

"Wait. I'm buying? Since when?"

"Since you offered, o' course! I don't know a single rich Irishman, and if my jumper's of good weave, that's because I knitted it myself." Gallows's signature woolen sweater was the color of cream and ribbed with artful cabled patterns. The Irishman reached to Bert's suit lapel, rubbing it between thumb and forefinger. Gallows waggled his light brown eyebrows and emitted a whistle of appreciation. "Nice, this! You never wore it before."

"Don't distract me. I never offered to buy — until now. I'll be happy to buy a round, but *after* I find this office I'm looking for, if you please. I'm almost two days late, thanks to the engines."

"And what's your business, Bert? What business could be more important than exercising your elbow?"

"Tungsten, molybdenum, and titanium, if you must know. Rare metals, but, apparently, useful for building airplanes."

"They have — them things — in Juneau?"

"Hopefully. Access to the ores, anyway. What is it you do for a living, Gallows? And what's your actual name?"

"Me? I live by my looks! The ladies feed me whenever I give 'em the piteous eye."

"Oh, stop." Bert shook his head, then scanned left and right. He spoke low, "Say, have you heard of a … ghost ship that sails these waters?"

The amiable expression on Gallows's broad face faded to an expressionless mask. "So ye've seen it, eh? The ghost liner? When?"

Bert's eyes lit up. "After you went to bed and I went on deck. It came out of the mists, and it didn't make a sound except for some click noises. No smoke, no engine noise, no sails. No wind anyway, even if it had six sheets hoisted. A minute later, it was gone."

9

"A passenger liner with no living soul aboard. Filled with gold and silver." Gallows's voice sank low with reverence.

"Well, I saw a little silver inside the portholes. Candlesticks and serving urns and such. Up on deck was a man or ghost. He stood on one leg, the only leg he had, still as if carved from granite." Even in the retelling, Bert felt his skin prickle with goosebumps. "His face stared forward, but I swear his eyes swiveled to follow me the whole time."

The two men stared at each other, attuned to the mystery, but a shout from the crew broke the mood. Their ship, the *Kodiak Minnow*, nudged against a dock. The smell of fish clogged the air as the crew lashed the ship snug and lowered the gangplank.

"Let's finish our talk at the pub, shall we?" Gallows said.

"I have to visit this mining office, first. I'll have to meet you."

"No need for that, my friend. I'll escort you. Which office did you say?"

"Morgan Mine Co."

"Aye. 'Tis on Silver Street. I'll show you."

They shouldered their baggage and waddled down the gangplank. Gallows led the way, threading a path off the docks and into the ramshackle town. The gold rush was long over, and the streets had an empty feel. Whether occupied or abandoned, every structure seemed composed of mossy wood capped by rusted tin roofs. The town smelled of snails and mildew. Past efforts to pave the streets had succumbed to ruts and potholes. Gallows led them between a pair of buildings. The gap between green-stained walls was narrow.

Bert hitched his bag to his other shoulder. "Wasn't that a pub we just passed? You seem to know your way around Juneau. Do you know where— Oh, sorry."

Gallows had stopped abruptly, and Bert almost ran him over. Gallows dropped his bag and began digging into it. "I'd just like to say," Gallows said to his bag, "that you're a capital fellow, Bert, and I wish there was another way."

Bert wrinkled his brow. "What?"

Gallows whirled and clipped Bert's skull with a blackjack pulled from the bag. Bert staggered two steps back, then dropped in a heap.

Gallows began searching Bert's clothes, starting with his wallet, from which he removed the cash. The Irishman tucked the money away and starting rifling through Bert's luggage.

A clearing of a throat arrested his movements. Gallows's head snapped up like a lad caught with his hand in the cookie jar. He found himself staring into the dark hole at the end of a Winchester rifle. "Oh. You?"

"Gallows. Tsk," the owner of the gun said. "You've done something rash. But I expect we can come to some understanding."

CHAPTER 2

Young Gilbert Fernwood stood by the hangar, hands clasped behind his back. His dark hair contrasted with the white of his flight suit. A sedan approaching at breakneck speed interrupted his skyward gaze. He managed not to flinch as the speeding car screeched to a halt only yards away from him. His eyebrows scrunched together in suspicion.

Four men piled out of the car in frantic haste. The four resembled escapees from the circus. Red hair flamed atop the broad one whose massive shoulders and chest threatened to burst his shirt and tweed coat. The short, paunchy one with dark skin sported a tiny black mustache with curled ends. The beanpole with tooled leather boots and a Stetson on his head looked as if he had been stretched out on a tanning rack, so tall and lean was he. Number four's normal body proportions seemed out of place amongst his companions. That one sported blond hair and a natty suit.

The men approached the lad with such urgency they might be contemplating violence. But Gilbert was fazed neither by their motley appearance nor their haste. His concern lay in the fact that they were there at all. The foursome should be in New York, but here they were at the Lark Haven, Pennsylvania airfield. Carroway Aeronautics occupied a cluster of hangars at one end of the airport. Two of the hangars were longer than football fields and ten stories tall. They both contained silvery dreams in the making: airships under

13

construction. A third, completed airship sat hangarless next to the others.

"Gilbert!" the blond man said. "Where's Ace?"

The young man pointed to the blue sky.

Necks craned, and all eyes speared upward. Two airplanes traveled the sky lanes, one tailing the other. The distant shapes flew perilously close together, or so it seemed.

Gilbert explained, "The engines aren't ready, but Ace is testing the body of the new plane. The second plane is the glider, the first one is a trimotor. They should cut the tow line soon."

It happened as Gilbert spoke. The airplanes separated. Ace's veered to the right.

"Is Lady Ace in control?" The short, plump fellow nervously stroked the curls of his black mustache. He was known as Sam in the group, a noteworthy fact because "Sam" was his actual first name.

"Aw, shucks, Sam. That's Ace up there," said Tombstone, the tall, bony Texan.

"Is that a yes or a no?" chuckled the handsome blond man, whose nickname was Quack. His tailored white suit accentuated his trim physique.

"Mostly a yep, I guess," Tombstone said, reaching up to resettle his Stetson on his head. Bas-relief cacti and tumbleweeds decorated his boot leather and shone with mink oil.

"Yew are a paragon of commitment, Tombstone," the broad fellow commented in Cockney accents. His name was Gooper, and his drooping mustache and hair blazed orange-red, in contrast to his pale face. His powerful chest strained against his shirt and tweed jacket.

"By the way, nice to see you again, Gilbert," Quack said.

"Welcome to Lark Haven," the lad said.

Ace's plane looked like no plane ever had before. Its wings swept back like those of a swallow. Its outline permitted no straight line, only graceful curves. Tucked under each wing, two empty metal barrels substituted for future engines.

The plane seemed to fall, then it rolled three times in quick succession. Sam sucked in his breath in alarm, but after the third inversion, the spin ceased. The wings stayed horizontal as if glued flat.

"Bee-ootiful," Gooper said.

Quack emitted a long whistle of appreciation. "I see what she is doing. It's daring maybe, but not crazy. It's like she's playing Chopin on a piano in a music store. She's finding out if the piano can keep pace with her fingers."

"An excellent analogy, sahib," Sam said.

Ace's plane descended quickly. It gleamed in silvery bronze as it rode an invisible helix to the end of the runway. The wheels chuffed as the plane touched down, bringing home the fact that it was a glider, flying silently, falling artfully.

The four stood mesmerized. They didn't realize that Gilbert had left them until they saw the lad atop a small tractor putt-putting from the hangar out to Ace's rolling plane. They scrambled to catch up on foot, converging on the airplane as it coasted to a stop only fifty yards from the hangar door.

The cockpit cover slid back, and a trim figure vaulted out. She touched a foot to the top of the wing and bounced to the tarmac. Between leather cap and flight suit, the skin of her face shone like burnished gold. Ace raised the goggles off her golden-hued eyes and grinned at the approaching gang. The sunny expression pulled at four parallel scars that raked at an angle across her temple and cheek.

"Hello, there, fellas! Tell you what, she maneuvers like a dream. But lift-wise, she flies like a soggy brick."

"Ace!" Quack blurted. "Bert's gone missing in Juneau."

Ace's smile compressed to a grim line. "So that's why you're all here. Tell me what you know."

"Yew tell 'er, Quack," Gooper said.

Quack blew air into his cheeks, then inhaled deep. In his rich baritone and all in one breath, he said, "Morgan Mining called. Bert's steamer was two days late, and the captain swears Bert was alive and well when they put in to Juneau. But Bert never came to the company office or checked into any of the hotels. The sheriff was notified but hasn't done anything so far, and that's all the fellow knew."

"And you drove all the way from New York to tell me?"

"It seemed the fastest and surest way," Quack said.

Gooper waggled a thumb in Quack's direction. "The way 'e drives, it's a wonder me lunch stayed down."

Tombstone said dourly, "I don't think there's any big rush. Sure as Kansas got corn, it'll be a girl. He got tripped up by a purty ankle."

Ace furrowed her brow at Tombstone. "Maybe, but if so, she acted fast and tripped him hard." She called to where Gilbert worked to attach the tractor to the front wheel of the glider. "Gilbert, how soon can *Sky*

Arrow One launch?"

He straightened up. "An hour or so, ma'am. The tanks are empty."

"Squeeze that hour into half an hour, if you can. Get Vivian and prep the airship. I'll stow the jet."

"Yes, ma'am."

GUY WORTHEY

18

CHAPTER 3

Captain Stone of the *Kodiak Minnow* choked on his coffee.

The sudden shadow that fell over the steamer could have been a cloud. The hum of engines overhead could have been another malfunction in the boilers or pistons. But a rope ladder dangling down from the sky, and a lithe figure dropping from it to land in loose-kneed nonchalance not five yards in front of the good captain, well, that would be enough to confuse anybody's windpipe.

Stone bolted from the wheelhouse to gape up at a looming oblong shape, as long as the *Kodiak Minnow* or longer. The dirigible matched the *Minnow*'s southbound course, but it glided in the air instead of the water. The flank of the airship gleamed in the sun, and the words *Sky Arrow One* crisply marched across its bow.

"Captain Stone, I presume?" a dry, amused female voice said.

The captain snapped his head back level. A woman in a flight suit and cap stood in a wide stance facing him directly, fists on hips. She was so tall she looked down on him. Gold-colored eyes competed for attention with a diagonal rake of scars across her face. Her magical materialization did nothing to soothe the captain's astonishment, but he managed an "Aye, aye, that's me," between coughs.

"Cecilia Carroway." She doffed her leather cap to reveal a disarray of gold-brown hair. Deftly, she

19

stuffed the cap and attached goggles under her wide belt for safekeeping. "I need your help, captain. You and your crew seem to be the last people to have seen Hubert Bostock. You probably called him Bert. He was a passenger on your last run up to Juneau."

The captain cleared his throat mightily. "Eh? I mean, uh, all right. I mean, the people from Morgan already talked to me before we sailed. The passengers were all healthy and happy, that I can tell you. The steward said this Bert fellow left with another passenger right after we docked."

"Which passenger?"

As they talked, the entire crew gathered around, wide-eyed and stepping gingerly: engineer, bosun, steward, and second mate.

"His name was Gallows," said the steward, a thick man with a pitted, reddened face. "Well, he signed his name with an 'X,' but we called him Gallows. An Irishman."

The mysterious visitor inclined her head. "Thank you. May I see your passenger list?"

The steward glanced at the captain.

Stone nodded. "Aye, though I don't see how it helps. Bert left us in one piece. If he went and got himself lost in Juneau, well, it's none of our business. We delivered him, fair and square."

"I'm not faulting you, Captain, just finding as much information as I can," Ace soothed. "I heard in Juneau you had engine trouble on the way up. It caused a delay."

The engineer wore suspenders and grease. He barked, "Ha! I'll say! The pistons are worn to a nubbin. They're looser than skin on an elephant. We try to fill the gaps with grease and chewing gum, but that can't go on much longer. We'll need parts once we dock in Seattle."

Ace said, "Was there anything else unusual during the northern leg?"

They all exchanged glances. Shoulders shrugged.

The bosun said, "Only the engine trouble. We had fog now and then, but generally the weather was fair."

That seemed to be the end of it. The steward escorted Ace to view the passenger log. Of the four entries, an "X" stood for Gallows. The other passengers signed H. E. D. C. Bostock III, Douglas Brown, and Watts Langley.

Ace studied the signatures, committing the handwriting idiosyncrasies to memory. As she straightened, she detected the mate hovering uncertainly outside the steward's cubby. He was an underweight fellow whose hands and ears seemed too big for his body. She said, "Hello. Did you remember something?"

The young mate's mouth twitched. He shuffled his feet.

Ace smoothed all brassiness out of her voice. "It's all right. Anything might help. We don't have a clue right now except that Bert's gone."

The mate winced, then nodded yes. "I overheard 'em, Gallows and the man you're looking for. Bert. Bert said he saw—" The mate swiveled his eyes left, right, and left again. He leaned toward Ace and whispered, "The ghost liner."

Ace blinked. "Oh? Do tell."

"What's more, I think another passenger, Watts, I think he overheard it, too."

"All right, but tell about this ghost liner."

21

"Well," the sailor hushed even more, so that Ace was reading lips more than she was comprehending actual speech sounds. "I only know this because I went to the Nugget one night. That's a poor excuse for a pub outside Juneau. I went hoping for cheaper drinks. They're cheaper, but I think they water 'em down."

Ace said, "I don't drink, myself. Tell me about the ghost liner."

"I'm getting there, ma'am. I overheard the Hapennys talking about it. Abel and Bette, I think their names are. They came out to Juneau a couple years back to stake a claim. The *Kodiak Minnow* brought 'em up. I remember because it was my first or second run between Seattle and Juneau. Or was it Sitka? Maybe it was one of those times we only made it to Ketchikan."

Ace gave him a withering look.

"Sorry, ma'am. Well, the Hapennys hushed their voices, but I got sharp hearing. They said their claim was a bust, but they heard about this ghost liner. It only sails at night, and it never makes a sound. No living soul sails her, just ghosts. And it's rich, like a rich man's yacht. Full of silver, they said. Full of gold. It's not a giant liner like the Queen Mary, I guess, just a regular steamer or a big yacht."

"Interesting. Anything else?"

"Not really. They debated back and forth if it left a wake or not. They decided it did. So it's real. They want to find it for the gold and silver. Makes sense. They came to Juneau for gold. They just got here forty years too late."

"All right, thanks for all that. I've two leads, now. Up from zero, which a good thing. Gallows the Irishman and this couple. What do they look like? Where are they from?"

The mate rubbed his freckled jaw. "They're both on the short side, brown or black hair. I guess they're maybe from the lower forty-eight. Don't really know."

"All right. One more thing. Did Bert say when he encountered the ghost ship?"

The mate answered readily. "The night before we landed in Juneau. The engines quit again. That was about midnight."

"What time did they get the engines going?"

"Five in the morning, I heard."

"And you reached Juneau when?"

"About eleven a.m."

"And what's cruising speed for the *Minnow*?"

"Seventeen knots."

"Good man. Thank you, friend."

CHAPTER 4

Ace signaled to the airship by waving her arms, and a rope ladder dropped and bounced. The young woman hooked a rung with a sinewy hand and clambered into the sky. Her unruffled expression implied that, for her, aerial acrobatics bordered on the humdrum. In less than a minute, she disappeared into the gondola.

The unhurried airship rotated and climbed, heading north once again. The crew of the *Kodiak Minnow* gazed after the airship until the silver flying needle pierced some low clouds and vanished.

On board *Sky Arrow One*, in the lounge behind the control room, Ace retold the ghost liner story. Her associates occupied various chairs.

"That's a bunch o' hooey," Tombstone grumped.

Gooper pointed a meaty finger at Tombstone. "*You're* a bunch of hooey, if hooey is something fed through a noodle machine and then dried crispy."

"Watch yer mouth, ya ginger gorilla."

"Straw-shaped hayseed."

"Blubbery varmint."

Ace dropped into a chair and waggled a finger. "Not now, fellas."

Tombstone and Gooper settled down, but they slid their eyes sidelong to Ace. Each pointed a finger at the other and silently mouthed, "He started it."

Young Gilbert Fernwood crossed the lounge, still clad in a white flight suit. "Coffee, anyone?" he called.

"Yes, please," piped a female voice from the helm. It was Vivian. She twisted in her seat and locked brown eyes with her twin brother.

He sniffed. "Naturally, *you*." He glanced around. "Anyone else?"

He got no other takers and sent Vivian a grimace before heading to the tiny galley tucked behind the lounge. Despite their tender years, the twins had crewed *Sky Arrow One* since before it was built.[1]

Ace drummed her fingers on the armrest of her seat. "I don't know if this ghost liner is a clue we should pursue. If we do, the last sighting was 120 miles south of Juneau among the islands of the inside passage."

Tombstone raised his Stetson an inch and rubbed his forehead. "How do ya figger that, Ace?"

"I worked it out from the timing as reported by the second mate. The fellow had a good head for detail, even if he tended to run on at the mouth."

Sam pulled at his starched collar with a finger. "I'm happy to *not* see a ghost ship, Lady Ace."

"You may not have to, Sam. There are other clues to check. For example, Bert left the ship with an Irishman called 'Gallows' who signs his name with an 'X.'"

Gooper's eyes widened, and he blew a rude sound from beneath his mustache. "An Irishman? Bugger all."

Quack chuckled. "Gallows? And here I was, think-

---

[1] We have no space in these pages to describe the adventure that united the Fernwood twins with Captain Carroway and her motley crew. Suffice it to say that it involved the chemistry of coal, a piano lesson, spies, and the rescue of their kidnapped mother.

ing 'Quack' was a prejudicial nickname! Mine's not so bad, after all."

Ace steepled her fingers. "The instant we land in Juneau, we should fan out to the various hotels and pubs. We need to find this Gallows fellow and interview him."

Muscles rippled along Quack's square jaw. "Yes."

"I have more names," Ace said. "Douglas Brown and Watts Langley were passengers on the *Kodiak Minnow* along with Bert. The mate also mentioned Abel and Bette Hapenny. They're prospectors in Juneau, but they haven't struck gold. They may be planning to turn pirate on the ghost ship, assuming it exists."

Vivian's young voice called from the control room, "Fogbanks are getting thicker, Captain Carroway. It's fifty-fifty on reaching Juneau before Juneau disappears."

They reached Juneau before the fog closed in completely. The sun set into the banks of low cloud, sending its last rays to illuminate the descending airship, painting its silver skin the hue of burnished gold. The only landmarks visible were treetops and a few scraggly telegraph and electric poles. The dirigible settled among trees that grew in Evergreen Cemetery, where the founders of Juneau, Richard Harris and Joe Juneau, lay interred.

Barely had *Sky Arrow One* settled among the marble markers when Ace and four men burst from the gondola. Sam paired with Quack, and Tombstone partnered with Gooper. Ace formed a team of one. Each team pocketed a scribbled list of destinations and a street map of Juneau. Each also carried a briefcase like a lawyer's. But the slim little cases contained no legal documents. Instead, each was a radio transmitter.

They dodged headstones as they jogged. The fog allowed only a few yards of visibility, and night was falling.

Gooper and Tombstone split from the group and headed for the southern end of town. In the fog, the pair resembled a celery stalk keeping company with a potato. To keep their bearings in the mist-wrapped gloom, they watched every street sign and tracked their location on the map. Gooper grinned and tapped a signpost as they passed. "Goldbelt Lane an' Gold Avenue. Methinks I detect an 'istorical theme."

"Yer a regular Ace Carroway fer deducin' that, Gooper." Tombstone tapped his paper list. "Look fer the Harris Hotel. We orta be close."

"I discern the 'otel's shingle, past yon stable. Not fancy, is it? Unpretentious cube of an edifice. If me eyes don't deceive, there's modern electric illumination interior."

"You mean they got a light bulb on inside."

Gooper's mustache bristled. "'At's wot I said!"

The unlikely pair shouldered into the shabby lobby. A desk clerk in visor and vest perked up and gushed, "Gentlemen! Need a room? We've got a vacancy."

"Howdy, pardner," Tombstone said. "We're jes' lookin' fer a feller. Goes by the name o' Gallows."

"He checked out." The clerk's face fell for a moment, then brightened up. "But he may be back in this fog. Can't sail in fog like this, nosirree!"

"Sail?" Gooper prompted.

"Oh, yessir! The Irishman was always on about his new boat. He said he'd got her stocked and was off hunting. Hunting was the word he used, sirs, not fishing. Maybe he meant hunting on the islands, but you can't sail in murk like this, nosirree."

Gooper stroked his bushy red droop of a mustache. "'At's a good point, mate. Did 'e say th' name of his boat? Or which slip she might be tied to?"

The clerk considered the question. "Well, sir, he left a forwarding address, but may I ask a question?"

"Sure thing, pardner," Tombstone said.

"You're not, erm, angry with the gentleman or anything? Not going to hurt him?"

"Nope. Never met him." Tombstone scratched at the stubble on his jaw.

"Ah. Good. Well, I was worried, is all."

"Worried?" Gooper said.

"The man, Gallows, was spending money fast. I just, you know, don't want a big spender hurt."

Tombstone grinned big. "Feller, I can see what you really mean. You're nervous that his money's ours, and we're trackin' him down to get it back."

The clerk's Adam's apple bounced as he swallowed. "Very perceptive, sir. But maybe his rich aunt died. People can come by money in a lot of ways."

Gooper nodded sagely. Paradoxically, his battered, bewhiskered face often instilled sympathy rather than fear. "No worries, guv. Now wot about that forwardin' address?"

"Right. It's slip nine at the marina."

♠ ♠ ♠

A moment later, outside the hotel and cloaked in dusk and fog, Tombstone slid a radio out of its leather case and extended the antenna. He placed it in Gooper's meaty hands and flicked the toggle to connect the battery.

Gooper patiently steadied the transmitter while Tombstone clapped a headset to his ear and keyed the call sequence. "Tombstone t' *Sky Arrow*. Come in. Over."

Gilbert's voice crackled back, "*Sky Arrow One* receiving. Over."

"Got a location for Gallows. It's a small boat at slip nine at the marina. We'll go there next. Got all that, Gilbert? Over."

After a delay, the radio crackled again, "Slip nine at the marina. Got it. Over."

"Good job, Gilbert. Over and out."

Tombstone stowed the headset, retracted the antenna, disconnected the battery, and stuffed the metal box into the case.

The case emitted a metallic clatter, and Gooper said, "Don't break those pulse transmitters, you clumsy overgrown twig."

"They're built tough. Unlike you, ya big wordy blob."

"Throw a punch at me, stick man. I'll show you whole new levels of tough."

"Cow patties." Tombstone snorted in derision. "Move them stubby legs faster. The marina's back north."

Chapter 5

Tied to slip number nine, a weary fishing trawler sloshed in the sluggish channel waves. Gooper squinted at the stern. "Oi think it says, '*Prince of Wales.*' Well, wot d' y' know?"

"Not a lot about Wales," Tombstone said. "I thought we was huntin' fer an Irishman. Ireland's not the same as Wales. Uh — right?"

Gooper laid a hand on his heart. "Tombstone, I will nobly forgive your embarrassing an' ignorant gaffe. Wales is part of England an' 'as been since the reign of King 'Enry the Eighth."

"Yessir, Perfesser Lumpy."

Gooper widened his stance and held up a finger, warming up to an impassioned oratory. "Ireland, on the other 'and, while also part of the British Commonwealth, is full of stubborn louts wot are currently rebelling against the crown." He jabbed his index finger in Tombstone's direction. "Compared to the lot of them, you yourself, subhuman miscreant though you are, come out smellin' like a rose an' lookin' like an angel."

Tombstone eyed Gooper as best he could in the foggy gloom and rubbed his unshaven chin. "What's your beef with Ireland? Ya got a burr under your saddle all of a sudden? We're half a world away from all that, here in Alaska."

"Yew 'ave, in the words of the poet, touched a

nerve," Gooper said in aggrieved tones.

"Well, paint me red an' call me a cow barn. Guess I have."

A new voice spoke in rolling Irish accents. "Gentlemen, if I could get a word in …"

Tombstone and Gooper swiveled to face the boat. An indistinct shadow on board resembled the outline of a man.

Tombstone tipped his hat. "Howdy, there."

"To what do I owe the pleasure of this visit?" The blurry shape hopped over the gunwales to alight on the timbers of the pier. As it approached, the blurry image sharpened until a man with sandy hair emerged. A knitted sweater cozily clad his torso from broad shoulders to trim waist, and a quizzical expression twisted his eyebrows.

Gooper answered, "We're lookin' for a friend of ours, wot's gone missing. Are you Gallows?"

"Gallows? I be he." Suspicion colored the Irish accents. "And who's your missing friend?"

Gooper said, "Dark-haired bloke named Bert."

"Bert, you say? Not the sharply dressed Bostonian?"

"That's him, rightly enough, pardner."

Gooper said, "Our inquiries so far indicate that yew were the last to see 'im."

"Missing, is he? Now, that's a surprise. He seemed in fine fettle when we arrived in …" Gallows spread his palms up to indicate the weather and rolled his eyes. "… sunny Juneau."

Tombstone said, "Tell us th' whole story, if you'd be so kind. I'm Tombstone. This here's Gooper. We jes' want to find our buddy, so anything you can tell us'd be greatly appreciated."

A crisp contralto interjected, "Tell me, too."

A tall figure materialized out of the mists between the celery and the potato. Tombstone glanced back. "Howdy, Ace. Good timin'. This here's Gallows. Say, what's yer full name, pardner?"

The Irishman brightened up and moved a pace toward Ace. He swept a deep bow. "Oren O'Gallagher, at your service, m'lady!"

Gooper's face scrunched up into an expression of disgust, but Gallows had eyes only for Ace.

"Cecilia Carroway, Oren. Or should I call you Gallows?"

"Call me Gallows. Everybody does. But, bless me, Bert has some high-quality friends! How noble of you to come to his rescue."

"Dunno about 'noble,' but we're his buddies fer sure," Tombstone said. "Did he run into a purdy woman? That's what I figger."

Gallows tore his eyes off Ace to shake his head at Tombstone. "Perhaps, lad, but not that I saw. He and I left the ship and went to a pub for a drink. That's all. After the drink — just the one, I swear! — we parted ways. He had an appointment with Morgan Mining, as I recall."

"Aw, nuts. I guess I'm wrong, unless there are two Morgans and one of 'em is a woman with a funny last name."

Ace snorted. "Unlikely, Tombstone." She studied Gallows as best she could in the gloom. His eyes were probably hazel, hair light brown. Laugh wrinkles at the corners of his eyes put his age shy of thirty. She said, "Which pub?"

"Ah, that would be the Well-dressed Salmon, miss. The busiest pub in town, but also the best. I'd love to take you there, if I could, but I can't. As soon as the fog clears, I'm off to fish."

Ace said, "Is there anything else you can remember? Anything odd or suspicious at all?"

"Nay, lass. Bert seemed a fine gentleman. His only fault was his timid poker playing. He and Brown both. They refused to bet more than a nickel." He displayed empty hands. "I barely made enough to buy a sandwich."

Ace stepped a foot closer to the Irishman. "Any talk of a ghost liner?"

If he blanched, it was subtle. He shook his head from side to side. "Nay, but it sounds romantic. In Ireland, there are tales of ships that went down with all hands but still ply the waters when the moon is right. Lovely old stories, mostly meant to frighten children, I expect."

"Oh? All right. If you're sure." Ace stared intently.

Gooper faded in from the gloomy mists behind Gallows. Even Ace couldn't recall exactly when he'd faded *out*, but he was back.

Gallows bowed. "Sure as the Alaskan night is long, miss."

Gooper said in jovial tones, "We'll not keep you, then. You've got fog to watch. Oi 'ope it breaks up so you can sail."

Gallows bounced on the balls of his feet. "I thank you for the kind words, lad. May you find your friend, and soon."

After a city block of silent, uphill trudging, Ace tapped Gooper's elbow. "You planted a pulse transmitter in the boat?"

"That I did!" Gooper chortled.

"Wut?" Tombstone stopped dead for a moment, then scrambled to keep up. "Why?"

Gooper fluffed his mustache and painted a serene expression over his broad face. "Yew cannot trust an Irishman. Full stop."

Tombstone spluttered, "Jes' because there's a civil war in Britain? That's as loony as a cactus hairbrush."

"Tombstone," Ace said, "in this case, Gooper's right. According to the mate on the *Kodiak Minnow*, Gallows heard Bert's story about the ghost liner. But, just now, he denied it."

Tombstone's face scrunched up. "Well, polish my boots an' call me a Yankee! I done been fooled."

Gooper said, "Additionally, 'e said 'e was going fishing, but the 'otel clerk reported he was going 'unting. Like I said, you cannot trust an Irishman. Anybody want to lay a wager that this Gallows bloke is chasing the ghost ship?"

"No bet," Ace said.

"No bet. Ah'm losin' my touch. Bert didn't trip over a pretty ankle, an' I couldn't smell a liar. I'm not stickin' my neck out again."

"Carry on down the list, fellas," Ace said. "We still need a concrete lead on Bert."

"Right-o, ma'am," Gooper said.

But she was already gone.

The staff at the Well-dressed Salmon couldn't remember a visit by Bert or Gallows.

The evening of legwork wore on. Ace approached her last stop, a seedy shack called the Nugget. According to the mate on the *Kodiak Minnow*, this bar served watered-down beer. Here, the mate had overheard Abel and Bette Hapenny whisper about a ghost liner. The night dragged on, and the fog began to break up. Overhead, stars winked on and off as shreds of fog drifted by.

Ace swung a wooden door open and stepped into a dim space. Hunting trophies crowded the rafters and walls. The stink of formaldehyde wafted in the dead air. One man in buckskins hunched over a table, back to Ace. The only other man visible leaned behind the bar, wearing a vest and holding a polishing rag. A row of spotty glasses crowded the bar in front of him, but he seemed disinclined to rub any shine into them. After he ran his eyes over Ace, he slicked his hair back and grinned like a wolf grins to a rabbit. "Welcome to the Nugget! What's your pleasure?"

Ace asked the same question she had asked at the previous dives she had visited. "I'm looking for a few people. Can you tell me if you know them?"

"Why, sure! Just tell me what drink you want." The fellow's toothy smile widened.

Ace sighed and plopped two bits on the bar. "Whatever's on tap. Firstly, Hubert Bostock. Goes by Bert. Medium build, dark hair, dresses well, first visit to Juneau as of a few days ago, but went missing almost immediately. Does that ring any bells?"

The proprietor poured beer from a tap into one of the dirty glasses. "Nope! No well-dressed gents here, for sure. You some kind of pilot?"

"Yes, I'm a pilot. Next is Abel and Bette Hapenny. I was half hoping to find them here."

"Nope, they haven't been here in weeks. They went treasure-hunting. Here you go. Drink up."

Ace didn't touch her beer. Didn't even look at it. "Treasure-hunting?"

"That's right. They finally gave up on finding Red Robber's lost claim. That's all they talked about last year. Now, it's some kind of haunted ship. They've gone from crazy to crazier. Sit down. Relax. What's your name? I'm Bill."

"Cecilia. Who has seen this mystery ship?"

"Nobody I've met, and I meet just about everybody in my line of work. I bet it's a fogbank. Seen plenty of those shaped just like a ship." His grin contained tobacco-stained teeth. "C'mon, relax."

"Staying tense strikes me as good policy, actually. Heard of Watts Langley?"

"Uh, heard of him, yeah. He's — I think he's with the governor's office or something. He's been around at least a few years. Never met him. C'mon, now, drink up. That's my best ale, that is." The bartender's greasy smile deepened to a leer.

Ace leveled a severe glance at him. "Stop pushing."

"Hey, I'm just a bartender. My job is to relax people. Let 'em talk their troubles out. Take their cares away." Belatedly, he decided that the dirty glasses needed polishing and stuffed a rag in one. He kept his eyes glued to Ace as he pretended to clean.

Ace examined ceiling stains and counted mentally to ten. She forced her lips to curve upward. "I'm talking. See? Douglas Brown. What about him?"

"Douglas Brown? Yeah, he's here. Douglas? Douglas? Now, where'd he go?"

Ace narrowed her eyes and glanced back. The man in buckskins had disappeared. Bill the bartender craned his neck, peering past Ace to the darkest corners of the dark shack. "Brown? Is that you behind the moose head?"

A pair of booted human feet under the gigantic spread of antlers twitched.

Bill the bartender slapped his own forehead. "Drat! No, that's not Brown. His name's … uh … Johnson. Yeah, Johnson."

Ace scowled fiercely at the bartender and resisted an urge to grab the front of his shirt.

The booted feet sprinted for the door. Ace caught a fleeting impression of buckskin trousers and jacket, complete with fringe. Bushy sideburns cascaded down the jaws of the fleeing man.

He banged through the door.

Ace pushed off from the bar and pursued.

Bill yelled, "Hey!" but Ace did not pause. The clammy cold of the foggy night slapped her face bracingly as she, too, quit the Nugget at high velocity.

Ace heard more than saw her quarry, at first. The street was a broad mud track, and Douglas Brown's footfalls splatted as he pelted down the track. But Ace sprinted, too, and gained.

As she closed the distance, the briefcase full of radio gear became a bother. She took aim, then spun the case like a discus on a low trajectory.

The case struck the fleeing man in the knees, and his legs tangled. He almost recovered, but a rut caught his foot and he sprawled into the street.

Ace decelerated. Moonlight showed more clearly his bushy sideburns and bare chin and upper lip. Too late, the moonlight also showed a thigh holster. Brown drew his gun as he rolled over onto his back. He aimed at Ace's chest. With a flash of light, the gun popped.

The numbing impact slapped her left shoulder even as she aimed her kick. Her booted foot caught his gun hand with a fleshy thump, and the weapon sailed into the darkness.

"Ow!" Brown cried.

No lance of agony in Ace's shoulder materialized. Instead, a tingling, burning sensation brought a worried wrinkle to her forehead as her body slammed on his, driving the air from his lungs with a whoosh. In a moment, her steely hand gripped his windpipe, and her dangerous eyes bored into his.

Despite the brutal pressure on his throat, Brown didn't much fight back. He gasped for air like a beached fish but only stared up at Ace, eyebrows working in perplexity. His lips formed silent words. "Who … are … you?"

The burn in Ace's shoulder spread like fire down her arm and through her chest. She glanced down, expecting a gush of her own blood. But no blood stained her flight suit. Only a tuft of feathers sprouted from just below her collarbone. With her spare hand, she plucked and beheld a dart, her blood painting its tip. Even as her vision darkened, she sniffed at it.

Dizziness washed over her. Her vision blanked altogether. Her muscles relaxed, no longer obeying her will. Slowly, she collapsed on top of her quarry. She muttered, "Curare. Didn't. Expect. That."

CHAPTER 6

Sam and Quack arrived at the airship and knocked on the gondola door. A boisterous voice inside promptly sang out, "'Oo goes there? Friend or foe?"

Quack answered, "Good grief, Gooper. It's us. Let us in. It's late. I'm ... I mean, Sam is pooped."

"Truly, sahib," Sam said, "That statement is accurate."

The door opened, and cheerful golden light spilled out. Gooper's red mustache beamed sunnily at them. "Come in! Come in! Did you find anybody?"

Sam said, "Not in person. Three on our list are well-known residents of this region. Abel and Bette Hapenny are miners who have been here about three years. Watts Langley is somehow connected with the territorial governor's office, though no one could recall his official title."

Quack said, "Other than that, not a thing. How about you?"

They marched past the cabins to the lounge. Tombstone lay sprawled on a padded bench, snoring.

Gooper stroked his mustache. "We found Gallows. He's a shifty, no-good Irishman. We planted a pulse transmitter on his boat. But ..." The broad rugby center heaved a sigh that threatened to pop buttons from his shirt. "But he's probably just chasing the ghost ship."

"I see," Quack said. "Is Ace here?"

"Naw."

There was a moment of silence.

"When should we start to worry?"

There was another moment of silence.

The curls on Sam's mustache drooped. "We worry now, it seems. On the good side, I noticed that the fog begins to lift."

Quack said, "There is a bit of moon, too."

Gooper said, "And it's not a large town."

Sam nudged Tombstone. "Tombstone. Wake up, sahib."

"Huh? What's the matter?" Tombstone sat up and rubbed his eyes.

"Ace isn't back yet," Quack said. "What was the last place she was supposed to visit?"

"I'm supposed to remember that?" Tombstone said with irritation. "Oh, wait. I do remember. It's the bar called the Nugget. Last bar on the south side of Juneau."

"Pubs. Not bars," Gooper said. "A bar is a long metal object I'm going to bend over your head one day soon."

"Let's find Ace," Quack said. "If she's found trouble, that's unfair. *We* want all the trouble. Am I right?"

"Too right, guv. Off we go, then."

They piled out. Sam was last and locked the airship door. Abruptly, they were cold and nearly blind in the darkness. They shuffled among half-seen marble grave markers. Mists turned silver by moonlight still clung here and there, flowing languorously past the stone monuments of the cemetery.

Crack! A stick broke somewhere to their left.

"Wot's that?" Gooper whispered.

The four hushed and huddled closer, reaching out to each other. Whatever lurked to their left went unseen.

"Maybe it's nothing," Sam murmured.

As if in instant denial, a low grunt chuffed from the darkness. It was answered by several more such, some higher in pitch and some lower. The inhuman sounds gusted like breathy coughs.

The men clutched each other tighter. The sounds did not repeat.

Finally, Quack said, "It was Yata, the north wind."

Tombstone sighed. "Y'all, we have Ace's li'l electric torches in our pockets."

In studied silence, four men dug into their pockets. Four beams of light drew foggy paths through the night. Unnervingly, dozens of yellow dots gleamed back, arranged in pairs.

"Aiee!" Sam shouted. He fumbled, and his electric torch spun to the ground, its beam flashing from nearby headstones. Meanwhile, more gleaming eyes appeared. A rumble vibrated the turf, and the eyes began to bounce, drawing nearer. It was as if a tidal wave raced toward them, laced with glowing jellyfish.

"Hold tight," Quack barked.

Knees none too solid, the men stayed in a group. Shadowy animal outlines moved, topped by glowing eyes. The rumble resolved into the beats of hooves, growing louder. Pumping shoulders and bobbing triangular heads approached at breakneck speed, fiery eyes aglow.

The men hunched their shoulders, bracing for impact.

But the stampeding herd of deer parted in two, flowing around the huddled group in elegant choreography. The roar of thudding hooves crested, then diminished. A few stragglers leapt headstones to follow their herd.

And then they were gone.

"About gave me an 'eart attack," Gooper wheezed.

Sam retrieved his electric torch from the turf. "Sahibs, do you remember when I was moments away from execution by the pharaoh of Meroë-Inet?"[2]

"Shore do," Tombstone said.

Sam exhaled in a puff. "This frightened me more."

Quack said, "I can't argue with that. Come on, let's get to town."

They trudged on, this time using their electric torches to avoid tripping on marble grave markers.

Before they were clear of the graveyard, Tombstone raised his left hand like a cavalryman, ordering a stop. "What's that?"

The four men stopped and stared, arrested by a sight as inexplicable as the deer eyes but even more monstrous. Heaving its way through the clinging mists, an animal shape limped, as if in pain. Like a lumpy pyramid on four legs, it seemed headless and aberrant.

"Crikey, wot now?" Gooper said.

"It's …" Sam said.

A few more steps and a few seconds later, the disturbing vision resolved. It was two people, one supporting the other with both arms. The supporter staggered, and the supported wobbled without strength in the legs. The pair paused.

A male voice said, "Whoa, look at that. An airship. All right. I'm convinced."

"… It's Lady Ace!" Sam said.

---

[2] Related in *Ace Carroway and the Midnight Scream*.

Sure enough, the limp baggage resembled the formerly dynamic Ace Carroway.

Gooper, Tombstone, Quack, and Sam rushed forward. Sam said, "Lady Ace? What is wrong? What is the matter?"

Tombstone's eyes narrowed, and his dour expression deepened to a scowl. "Who's that varmint with her?"

Ace's voice slurred as she replied. Also, her face was wedged into the shoulder of her supporter, to the detriment of clear speech. "Fellash. Thish ish Douglash Brown. Our assoshiation shtarted off awkward, but thingsh are cozhier now."

Tombstone and Gooper flanked Ace and claimed the job of holding her up. She would have fallen in a heap otherwise.

Quack's brow furrowed. "What now? Douglas Brown? What happened?"

"I'm Douglas Brown." The man rubbed his own arms, then swung them about and shook them. "Cecilia Carroway is heavy! Gentlemen, I do apologize. I drugged her. I was in a panic at the time. I should have thought out a better way, but I feared my cover would be blown."

"My head'sh all floppy," Ace slurred as she left a petite smear of saliva on Tombstone's leather jacket.

Quack said, "Cover? Blown? We'd better have this from the beginning. Come on, everybody, let's get Ace into the warmth. What can we do, Ace? What drug? Is there an antidote?"

Aboard *Sky Arrow One*, Ace's incoherent protests at being fussed over were ignored. Soon, she reclined in the gondola lounge, propped by pillows. She sipped water through a surgical pipette, which was the closest Vivian could come to a drinking straw on short notice. Water, Ace said, was the best remedy at this point.

Blotches of mud on Douglas Brown's buckskin outfit led him to arrange a towel on a chair before he sat. He was a man in his prime, with bushy brown eyebrows and distinctive prominent sideburns. He surrendered Ace's briefcase full of radio gear. The case had been dangling from his belt as he all but carried Ace a long half mile to the airship. Despite this hardship, he recovered his wind quickly. He glanced at Ace and wrung his hands, guilt lengthening his tanned face.

Gooper glowered at Brown. "Awright. Spill."

Brown's eyes strayed to Gooper's bulging chest and shoulders, but he displayed little nervousness. "I'm Douglas Brown, technically a private citizen at the moment. I will tell you my story, but only if you keep what I am about to tell you confidential. I fear that loose talk may put some in danger. I'd like your word of honor, if you please."

Ace said, her speech crisper by the minute, "As long as it's nothing illegal, done. You have my word."

"Aye."

"Yup."

"Yes, sahib."

"All right."

Brown exhaled. "Thank you. Well, here goes. I hope I'm doing the right thing by telling you. I'm on leave from the Royal Canadian Mounted Police. I was a constable and hope to be again once this business is over."

Quack said, "Are you going to get to the part where you drugged Ace? So far, your apology is not accepted as far as I'm concerned."

Brown lifted his chin. "I said it was a mistake. Miss Carroway came into that blot of a drinking hole and started dropping names, mine included. I could not speak openly in front of the bartender, and who Miss Carroway might be was not clear to me. I mean, I've heard of Ace Carroway — who hasn't? — but I wondered if she might be some imposter. Perhaps someone on the other side, so to speak. So I bolted before she could get a look at my face. When she ran me to ground, I shot her with a poisoned dart. I plead self-defense."

Ace said, "Fellas, I believe him, and I was there."

Quack said, "I guess I'll let it pass. All right. On with your story, then."

Brown inclined his head. "I salute your attitude, sir. But, yes, to continue. The reason for my leave of absence is related to the wreck of the *Sir John Thompson*, a Canadian ship lost during the Great War."

Ace broke off from sipping water. "That wasn't a warship, at first. They bolted a few guns on and converted it to a troop carrier."

"Yes. Very good." Brown steepled his fingers. "The ship disappeared shortly after the United States declared war. Canada had been at war for over a year already. The Alaskan territorial government reported a last sighting out to sea in the North Pacific. And there the matter rested for several years.

"Two things renewed our interest. The most direct was an anonymous letter from Port Clam, a little village south of here. The letter claimed that the *Sir John Thompson* sank here, in the inside passage, not out in the Pacific. The second oddity cropped up when we checked into the known facts. The report of the Pacific sighting was penned by one individual, territorial governor Adam S. Kleine."

Tombstone scratched his head. "Th' suicide governor?"

"Yes, that's the one. No details were stated, only the bald declaration that the *Thompson* had been sighted eastbound in mid-Pacific. It's quite impossible that Kleine himself witnessed such a thing."

"Wait. 'Oo, now?" Gooper asked.

Tombstone shifted his Stetson to scratch his narrow head. "Kleine was governor of the Alaska Territory when the Great War broke out. He made it no secret he sympathized with th' Ottomans or, at least, the Germans. When the States declared war, he shot hisself. A fit of despair, folks said."

Brown held up a finger. "Timing becomes important. Kleine had several days between receiving the news about the war and committing suicide. I checked dates. It was during this time he sent the letter about the sighting of the *Thompson*. Amidst these considerations, I was dispatched to attempt to find the writer of the anonymous letter."

Quack said, "But not officially. Undercover."

Brown said, "Exactly. This isn't Canada. I dressed in buckskins and pretended to be a hunter."

Ace said, "Did you find the author?"

"I did." Brown stroked his clean-shaven chin. "I came to Port Clam, population about fifteen, and interviewed the general store owner, who doubles as the postmaster, mayor, and garbage collector. She put me in contact with a native woman, the one who had written the note. She, in turn, guided me to the wreck. The prow was still above water. I saw the full lettering, *Sir John Thompson*, when I dunked my head underwater."

Ace mused, "Why would Kleine misstate the position of the ship? And how would he know? And why would he even care?"

Brown said, through tight lips, "I don't know, but *somebody* wants that ship to stay lost. Just after I saw the lettering, they started shooting."

CHAPTER 7

"What? As in actual bullets?" Quack said.

"Yes." Brown's expression turned rueful. "Tillamook and I — that was my guide's name, Tillamook — we were in a small motorboat. We sheltered behind the motor to escape the onslaught and headed directly away. The boat was holed, but we managed to make the far shore."

Sam said, "What a harrowing adventure, sahib!"

"That wasn't the end of it. A motorboat soon appeared, chasing us. More riflemen were aboard. We caught glimpses of them from among the trees. Lady and gentlemen, the rifles were recognizably German."

A low warble suffused through the lounge, coming from everywhere and nowhere, haunting and otherworldly. Brown looked around, confused. Everyone else looked at Ace. Her mouth unpursed, and the musical trill ceased. She sat up and shot a keen glance at Brown. "Don't mind me, I'm just surprised. The plot thickens. I presume you escaped in the end, Mr. Brown?"

Brown dipped his head in the affirmative. "We fled to the north on foot. We swam the next channel and the next. I gave Tillamook what cash I had as a down payment on the boat she had lost. I departed for Juneau, and she said she would go back to Port Clam, despite my objections. I'm not sure she will be safe there."

Ace began stretching her limbs, testing them. "Nor am I."

"As for me, from Juneau I arranged passage to Victoria to brief the office there. They were less impressed than you at my description of the chase, but they allowed me to outfit myself for the return journey. The dart pistol, for example. And diving equipment."

Ace raised her eyebrows. "You plan to dive at the *Sir John Thompson*?"

"I do."

"Yew got a death wish, guv." Gooper nudged the nearest person, who happened to be Sam. "Our type o' bloke, eh?"

Sam put out a stabilizing hand to prevent himself from being toppled. "Indubitably, sahib."

"What did you do after Victoria?" Ace said.

"I resumed my disguise and caught a steamer north."

"The *Kodiak Minnow* with Bert, Gallows, and Watts," Ace said, without a hint of a question in her tone.

"Yes, that's right. The voyage north stayed quiet, but it got rough again when I hit Juneau. I needed to hire a boat and go south, but it couldn't be done in a day. When I went to my hotel, it was being watched by a bearded fellow dressed like a trapper. He practically stared at me. My hackles rose, and I kept walking. Sure enough, he followed. After I lost him, I slept up in the hills."

"Interesting," Ace said. "Leaving aside the question of why, the fact that they had the manpower to track you the moment you arrive tells a lot."

Brown stared at her, not because of her words, but

because she had spoken them from a handstand position, perfectly inverted. As he watched, Ace floated one hand away. Balanced on the remaining hand, her legs and arms twisted in intricate, dancelike patterns.

Quack flapped a hand in front of Brown's eyes. "It's her exercises. Pay them no mind. She does them every day."

Brown blinked several times. "I see. Right. Where was I? Oh, Juneau. Well, they started guarding the boat I had rented. The bearded trapper and a second man bundled up in fisherman's rain gear. I couldn't leave. I managed to rescue my diving gear, though. It's stashed up in the woods."

"The telegraph?" Ace sat on the floor, pitting muscles against muscles with the goal of achieving conscious control over flesh normally moved by instinct alone.

"The telegraph is down," Brown said gloomily.

"That," Sam said, "is quite a coincidence."

"And if it's not a coincidence," Quack mused, "it's quite a conspiracy."

"I eyed the outside of the capitol building earlier today, but I couldn't bring myself to go in and beg for help. The thought entered my head that I should capture one of these spies and interrogate them. I was biding my time in the Nugget when Miss Carroway here walked in."

"And you shot her with a poison dart," Quack accused.

"I did. Before the bartender, as it turns out. He tried to sedate her, too."

Ace was on her feet, doing deep breathing exercises. "I wondered, but I didn't want to believe it. It seemed too loathsome to be true."

"I wish it weren't. If I were the sheriff, I'd investigate him in a hot second. He's a toad of man."

"Brown?" Ace opened her eyes and faced him squarely.

"Yes?"

"Do you know *anything* about where Bert might be?"

"Not a thing."

"All right. Fetch your diving gear. We'll give you a lift to the *Sir John Thompson*."

Chapter 8

Some hours later, *Sky Arrow One* cruised the skyways south of Juneau. Gilbert called from the control room, "We are passing over pulse transmitter five, now."

Gooper cooed and smacked a ham fist into his opposite palm. "The Irish blighter."

"What's this?" Brown's brow wrinkled. "Pulse transmitter five?"

Sam spindled one curled end of his mustache in satisfaction. "At Ace Carroway and Associates, we have advanced radio gear, sahib. The pulse transmitter sends dots once each second, and with a loop antenna, we can triangulate the location of said transmitter. Number five is the one Gooper hid aboard the boat driven by Gallows, which personage, we surmise, is chasing the ghost liner."

Brown blinked. "That's amazing."

Gilbert called again, "Visual contact, barely. Just a white seed on the water."

"Thank you, Gilbert," Ace said.

"Can we buzz him?" Gooper said eagerly.

"Down, boy," Tombstone said with a scowl.

"Ow, come on, where's yer sense o' fun? We could drop eggs on him."

"We could drop Gooper on him." Tombstone's eyes widened. "Say, wait a minute. Ah'm warmin' up to this idea."

Gooper's red mustache bristled. "I'll put the drop

on *you*, stork-legs."

"That ain't nearly as entertainin'." Tombstone's long face drooped mournfully.

But *Sky Arrow One* performed no aerobatic maneuvers. It glided south over the inside passage like a silver bullet through the air, silent and swift.

In the lounge, the associates and Douglas Brown hunched over a nautical map of the area. While the main waterways were marked with depths and coordinates aplenty, the land masses were featureless blobs. Brown couldn't even place Port Clam with confidence until he spotted its lighthouse on the map.

The undercover Mountie spread his hands in surrender. "I don't think even the shorelines are right. I'm sure there are inlets here and here." He pointed to the spots.

"It's a maze," Quack said. "Winding waterways and fingers of land mixed with true islands."

"Too tedious to chart properly, apparently," Ace agreed.

Brown said, "All I know is the general direction: southwest of Port Clam. We zigzagged a lot getting there."

Ace said, "We should try to find Tillamook."

Brown nodded eagerly. "Good idea! I'm worried about her."

Tombstone rubbed his long jaw. "What kinda name is Tillamook?"

Sam answered, "It is the name of a native tribe many miles south of here, at the mouth of the Columbia River. It is the name of a person, too?"

Brown's eyes drifted to the windows, but they did not appear to focus on the scenery. "She is known as

'The Tillamook.' Meaning a traveler far from home, perhaps. Or an outcast. If she had some other name, she never told me." His voice, too, sounded faraway.

As they talked, Ace held a caliper-compass to the scale on the map and dialed the separation to five miles. She inscribed a circle on the map, centered on the waters of the inland passage. She gazed at her marks speculatively. "On the topic of Gallows and the ghost liner," she said, "this might be of interest. I calculate that both Port Clam and the wreck of the *Sir John Thompson* are within a mile or two of where Bert spotted the spectral ship."

"Good," Gooper growled. "I want ter meet that Gallows again. 'E knows more about Bert than 'e's tellin', and I'm going ter beat it out of 'im."

Brown eyed Gooper's bulging arms and meaty fists.

Quack steepled his fingers. "I'll help, Gooper."

Brown cleared his throat. "May I ask why Bert Bostock was going to Juneau? Could it have anything to do with his disappearance?"

Ace said, "He was to arrange with Morgan Mining for delivery of elemental tungsten, molybdenum, and titanium to Pennsylvania."

Brown stroked his chin. "Sounds expensive."

Ace's lips curved in a lopsided smile. "Yes, in the quantities I want. But he carried only some papers, a checkbook, and traveling cash."

"He may look like a dandy," Quack put in, "but he's a scrapper in a fight."

Brown pursed his lips reflectively. "He looked like a dandy, all right. Not the sort of roughneck you'd expect in Alaska."

"He never arrived at Morgan Mining." Ace's eyes

strayed to the forward window. "We checked there before we intercepted the *Kodiak Minnow*."

Sam nodded vigorously. "The smelter was happy to provide tungsten and molybdenum, but they were out of titanium. The territorial government had bought it all."

Ace sighed. "I don't think I can finish my new engine without a good mass of titanium. But that's a problem for another day."

Clouds and mists layered the skies. The dirigible slowed as it approached Port Clam. All hands scanned for identifiable points of reference but saw only glistening watery paths and forested ridges. Vivian sat straight-backed at the helm as her twin brother craned his neck at one of the many windows.

Sam stabbed his finger downward. "The lighthouse. I see it."

Ace followed his point. "Forty degrees starboard, Vivian. Pitch ten degrees down and decrease lift. Maintain slow."

"Yes, ma'am."

The sleek airship nosed downward and felt its way through the mists as a light rain began to fall. Only rare patches of forested ground showed themselves through the fog, and finding a landing place became guesswork. Ace picked a ridge inland from the flashing lighthouse. The ridgetop pine trees grew lushly, but they were only a few years old and a dozen feet tall.

"Spooky," Quack murmured as he watched the mists swirl like ghostly octopus tentacles.

The airship nestled into the trees, with woody scrapes and squeaks. The descending gondola bent several trees flat. The remainder of the young conifers reached just high enough to tickle the silver dirigible's skin with their feathery needles.

Like the distributor cap in an engine, Ace fired off instructions to her crew: the pistons in the Carroway and Associates machine. "Vivian, compress the lift gas, then kill the engines and go electric. Quack, Sam, and Gooper, the last closet on the right has a few tools, including a hatchet. See if you can clear a path and tie the airship down. Gilbert, stay on the radio. We'll be calling in from time to time. The rest of you, pack for the wet. We'll add our own diving gear to Brown's. First stop, Port Clam. After that, we'll chart our next moves."

Ace eyed her associates one by one. "Gallows can probably see well enough to navigate. I expect he'll be docking in about two hours, if he docks at all. Tombstone, bring your long rifle. Everybody, keep sharp. German infantry rifles lurk here, somewhere. Vivian? Go easy on the electricity. That means no hot coffee."

"What?" Vivian started in guilt, then her face drooped. "I mean, yes, ma'am."

Hulda Gustafsdottir gave the simmering chowder a stir. With the weather worsening, the fishermen would be back early. She looked around the trading post possessively. It wasn't perfect, but it was hers. Nabbing a potholder, Hulda slid the heavy iron lid back on the iron kettle.

The front door creaked open. She called over her

shoulder, "Arni? What took you so long?"

But a female voice answered in American accents, "Hello. If Arni's the young fellow stacking firewood, I'm sure he'll be along in a moment."

Hulda spun around, all rosy cheeks and smile wrinkles. She dusted off her apron. Her eyes widened and her smile broadened as she beheld the incoming damp parade. Strangers all, they seemed like characters. A tall woman with scars on her face led a clump of assorted men. "Visitors! Oh! A lot of visitors! Come on in. Chowder's hot, if I can tempt you with that."

Tombstone tipped his Stetson. "Thank you, ma'am. I think we might be more interested in chewin' the fat."

"Bone boy," Gooper said, "that was an 'orrible mixed metaphor. If not stew, wot fat were you goin' ter chew, then?"

Tombstone scowled. "I meant we wanted to talk, is all."

In the meantime, Hulda counted, "Four. Five. Six!" Her face darkened. "Oh. *You*. Brown." Severely, she said, "You need to leave. Now. Not all of you, just Brown."

The group stopped and shuffled, eyeing each other and Hulda.

Brown said, "Wasn't planning on staying, Hulda. Did Tillamook come back?"

The agitated proprietor seized a pair of tongs from beside the wood-burning stove and shook them at Brown. "Can't say. Won't say. Can't say a thing. Not negotiable! You got to leave! Got to, I say!"

Ace held up a hand. "Hold on. Hulda, my name is Ace. We're leaving, no worries there. Just tell us where

Tillamook is."

Hulda froze, face fierce, tongs held high. For a moment, it seemed as if she might hurtle the iron implement at them. Instead, she slammed the tongs back into their place and stomped behind her merchant's counter. She seized the stub of a pencil and began to scribble on the back of a paper receipt.

With many curious eyes on her, she wrote and ranted, "You. Bah. No idea what you're doing. No idea. Me? I have no idea where Tillamook is. No idea if it's ridge one to the south. Or ridge two. Or around ridge three and up to the waterfall. Could be anywhere. Hulda doesn't know everything." Her soliloquy seemed more theatrical than sincere, but it kept the men and Ace bemused.

Abruptly, her voice quieted. "Don't take so many people. You'll scare her away for sure."

"Begone!" Hulda wailed and shoved her hasty sketch at Ace.

Ace glanced at the paper and tucked it into one of the many pockets of her flight suit. "Gooper, Tombstone, Quack, and Sam, you four stay. Give Gallows a warm welcome — by which I mean the opposite, of course. He's still our best lead on Bert."

Gooper's mustache curved upward. "We'll stay if we get ter interview Gallows."

Tombstone said, "Don't hog all the fun now, Ace."

The Brit blew air through his mustache. "Fat. Hogs. Wot's wif all the blubber language, beanpole?"

Ace leveled a pointer finger at Tombstone. "Be ready for anything. I've got a pinger in my pocket." Ace pivoted and sketched a two-finger salute toward Hulda. She made shooing motions toward the door.

"Come on, Mr. Brown. Time to disappear."

Chapter 9

Ace emerged into the dank drizzle. A young man labored in the shed adjacent to the trading post, splitting logs with wedges and a hammer. He shared Hulda's round features and rosy cheeks. Ace strode toward the youth, Brown in her wake.

The lad's head snapped up, and his mouth dropped open. The golden flier filled his vision, face vividly scarred. Placid she seemed, yet at the same time, she exuded an electric aura of immediacy.

"A dollar to you, Arni," the female apparition said to the flabbergasted youth, "if you tell me who frightened your mother."

He blanched. His eyes darted left and right for an escape route.

"Whisper it," Ace cajoled. A green paper corner poked above her carefully cupped hand.

"You. You'd better just go … Oh, a whole dollar?"

Ace adjusted the green paper until the letters "ONE" appeared. "Please?"

"You win, stranger. Next time I get over to Juneau, I can … oh, so many things."

"You can. So who's your mom afraid of?"

"It's the swamp men," Arni whispered.

Ace's eyebrows shot up. So did Brown's as he hovered behind her shoulder.

"They always come to Mother for supplies. In the night. For years, now. Always secret. I heard them a few nights ago, past midnight, talking with Mother.

She trembled after that and told me to shut up. Now give me my money!"

Ace said, "Almost. Where do these swamp men come from?"

"Don't know. Now get out of here and give me my money."

"Why do you call them swamp men, then?" Ace kept her money and narrowed her eyes.

"Oh. I peek, sometimes. They dress in green suits like … well, like yours, except blotchy green and brown." Arni gestured with his hammer at Ace's flight coveralls. "And all over the suits they hang moss. All over. And they paint their faces green, too. Moss on their helmets. Will you get out of here?"

"Interesting. Yes, we'll go now."

Arni snatched the offered bill and stuffed it away in his trouser pocket.

Sam made a salaam to Hulda. "Greetings, milady. I am called Sam. This is our first visit to Port Clam."

"You don't say," Hulda said, her mouth a flat line. "I am Hulda Gustafsdottir, owner of this general store. Would you like some crab chowder? Two bits a bowl."

Quack said, "No, thank you. We need to get to the dock to … meet a friend."

Tombstone's face resembled a mournful basset hound. "Aww, shucks. I was lookin' forward to a hot bite."

Gooper grinned. "Hog."

Tombstone gritted his teeth. "You're the hog, you lump o' lard."

Hulda's eyebrows worked. "Another friend? How many are a-comin'? Port Clam is no Seattle! We might not have enough beds in the whole town."

"I'm sure you won't have to find beds for us, ma'am," Quack said. "Come on, you lot. Let's go meet Gallows."

They filed out into the drizzle, hunching their shoulders against the chill. As they filed out, the young wood-gatherer hovered near with narrowed eyes. He got grins and waves in return.

The associates shuffled down to the dock through the brown wet. No roads graced Port Clam. Only beaten tracks connected the haphazard cluster of houses. Nets, floats, and other cast-off tools of the fishing trade decorated the mossy wood structures. The light rain had washed away the densest mists, but visibility was still poor under the piles of heavy clouds.

Quack glanced at his compatriots. "What was all that about in there? I'm not sure I caught all the hints."

Tombstone shrugged. "The store owner seemed affrighted. She was scared of gettin' caught with Brown in her store. Scared of even sayin' anything."

"Why should she be scared?" Quack said.

"Scared o' lizard man's breath, mayhap," Gooper said.

Sam said, "I see a boat!"

"Already?" Quack spun and scanned the gray panorama. Eastward, the lazy flash of the lighthouse beacon winked. It sat on a jutting rock near the limit of their vision, blurred to shades of gray by the curtain of rain.

Between the lighthouse and shore, an approaching prow parted the waters into foam.

"He's early, I guess." Tombstone shrugged.

Sam cleared his throat. "Gentlemen. What is our plan?"

"Oi say we beat 'im black an' blue." Gooper's mustache smiled beatifically.

Quack sighed. "Gooper."

Tombstone muttered, "Bloodthirsty British blob."

Sam said, "Permit me to propose an alternate plan?"

"Go ahead, Sam," Quack said.

"Well, sahib, what if we were to simply occupy his boat? Our presence would destroy whatever he wished to accomplish. Surely, he will try lies for some time, to get us to leave, but we will not believe them."

"I like it," Quack said.

"Plus, we can search his boat," Tombstone said. "Iffen he's got somethin' to hide, inanimate objects can't lie."

Sam inclined his head. "The boat comes swiftly now." The burr of a gasoline motor grew loud, then cut low. The boat coasted toward the long dock.

Quack said, "Casual. Act casual. Maybe we're the Port Clam welcoming committee."

The four attempted to saunter as they shuffled forward in the rain to meet the boat.

A man in the boat held a loop of rope, which he threw over a post as the boat bumped the dock. The four rushed forward and swarmed aboard.

"Hey!" The sharp word contained no trace of Irish lilt.

CHAPTER 10

Ace led the way into the dripping trees until Port Clam disappeared, a matter of a few minutes. She next insisted upon using the radio tucked away in a backpack. Brown wore a backpack, too. Between them, they carried two diving suits and an air pump.

After she informed Gilbert that the party had split up, she retracted the antenna and closed the cover on the radio console.

Brown's scrunched face mirrored his impatient gestures. "Well? What's scribbled on that map? Where are we going? Will I be left in the dark forever? I'm not sure I like your style, Miss Carroway."

Ace remained unruffled. "Action is sometimes more important than full disclosure, but now we have a moment to talk. Hulda drew a map that does not resemble her verbal instructions at all."

Brown grunted. "She treated me like a criminal or something. We had gotten along well, before."

"I surmise she was fearful of eavesdroppers. Perhaps unreasonably, perhaps not. Certainly, *swamp men* who only visit in the dead of night could cause fits of nervousness."

"Swamp men." Brown's eyebrows scrunched together.

Ace fished out the marked-up sales receipt and handed it to the Mountie. He turned it this way and that, trying to make sense of the wiggles even as the drizzle obscured them further. "Well, 'PC' must be Port Clam, and maybe that's an island. But I don't recognize that symbol."

"I think she was trying for the pair of pickaxes. The symbol for mining."

"Oh, that would be the garnet hole. Tillamook mentioned it a time or two. A failed mine. It contains too few garnets to be profitable."

"Good." Ace stabbed a finger at the map. "If this way is north, and this is Port Clam, then here's the 'X.' We need to head straight west."

"It's steep that way."

"It's steep every way."

"Hey!" the man shouted. "What's the big idea? Who are you?"

A female voice piped up. "Get off our boat!"

The four associates froze and gaped. The man was short and dark-haired under his rain hood. The woman frowned ferociously at them from the wheelhouse. The boat was bigger than Gallows's *Prince of Wales*. Big enough to have a wheelhouse, though only barely.

"Oh, blimey. Sorry, guv. Sorry, Madame."

Quack said, "Pardon us. Case of mistaken identity. We were looking for a tall Irishman with light hair."

The man and woman both stared. Their boat drifted lazily, eventually coming to the end of its tether and gently sloshing. The rain pattered on wood and people.

The man said, "Not Gallows—?"

Gooper said, "The very same. Know the blighter?"

The woman's affronted facial expression transformed to outraged. "You expected to meet Gallows? Why? Why do you think he's coming here? Why do you think he's coming here *now*, of all times?"

Tombstone grinned. Many of his smiles tended to make his lean face more skeletal, but this one managed to translate as folksy and pleasant. "Tell you what. Let's do some introductions and we'll swap stories. I go by the handle Tombstone. This here's Quack. That's Sam, and that's Gooper. We're here because we think Gallows might know more than he's lettin' on about our friend Bert. Bert's gone missing, y' see. We're lookin' fer him."

The man climbed up next to his wife. "Huh. You don't say? Well, I'm Abel Hapenny. This is my wife, Bette. We're, uh, we're on a pleasure cruise. Just didn't expect to meet Gallows. We, uh, don't like him."

Sam said, "Sahib. Memsahib. I do not wish to be rude, but please allow me to contradict you on the matter of the pleasure cruise."

The pair goggled at the rotund Egyptian as if he were a fish that had flopped aboard and sprouted legs.

Sam continued with placid sympathy, "Generally, you see, people wait for good weather for such things. Allow me one further conjecture, which may help dispel the need for secrecy. If I may be so bold, you are here to search for a ghostly ship that sails in silence and sails only at night."

Both man and wife appeared as if they were attempting to swallow a fork sideways.

Quack spread his hands. "We're not interested in ghost liners. Well, I mean, we *are*, out of academic curiosity. But not like you or Gallows. We just want to find Bert."

"Gallows is a snake!" Bette hissed. "He'd better not jump our claim. That ghost ship is ours."

Abel jutted his chin out. "Swear you won't horn in on our claim?"

Quack pressed his right hand over his heart. "If it's salvage, it's yours. Bert's our only concern. Say, you don't know anything about Bert, do you? Hubert Ewing Devery Christopher Bostock III, of Boston. Disappeared four days ago in Juneau."

Both shook their heads. "Never heard of him."

Sam said, "Lady and gentlemen, another boat comes."

CHAPTER II

Ace and Brown journeyed doggedly, soaked to the skin and chilled to the bone. They were also more lost than not as they pushed through the dripping tamaracks, cedars, spruces, and pines.

"The day won't last much longer," Brown panted.

"True," Ace said.

The forest opened to the sky at a hummocky glade, gently sloped and dotted by only a few trees.

"There's the water, down there!" Brown pointed. Placid seawater rippled a hundred yards further on.

"We're close to the mine. I guess it's to the right." Ace paused and sent worried glances here and there. For a moment, she lifted her face to the rain. The droplets caressed her skin, and a relaxed half-smile stole over her features. But the next moment, worry bordering on alarm creased her brows, and she spun in place, eyes roving.

Brown regarded the performance with a dour expression. "You're quite the case, aren't you?"

The drenched pilot spared a glance for Brown as her eyes continued to search. "Yes, I suppose I am, Mr. Brown. I ... I haven't told anyone this in years, but ... I can feel the sun."

Droplets fell from Brown's prominent sideburns. "What does that mean?"

"It is a profound admission, because I can't explain it. I have a good memory because I work to improve it. I strive daily to become stronger and faster. I train to develop my skills. But this one thing I did not earn: I can feel the sun. It is there, right there, beyond the rain and cloud."

Brown shrugged.

Ace's teeth flashed white. "Good answer, Mr. Brown." Her expression tightened again. "But my extra sense fails me now. Shadows flit and frolic and bring shades of darkness and cold. The sun suffers. It comes and goes. I am cold."

The Mountie stared at her face. She seemed to have gone pale. He inhaled and blew air through puffed cheeks. "Well, that part's understandable."

Jolted out of her funk, she blinked at him. "How?"

"There are dark places, that's all. A woodsman knows. I've felt it for a little while now. This is a black-hearted dell, full of misery. Full of restless spirits."

"I do not believe in ghosts!"

"That's all right." Brown's voice carried a wistful tinge. "Ghosts don't need your permission to exist."

Ace sent a quelling glance to Brown, then a yearning one toward the spot in the sky where she knew the sun floated. A shadow passed, or seemed to, and her eyes followed the absence of sunlight down as it dove to the grass and weeds. There, the tiniest of metallic glints caught her eye. She blinked. She moved forward.

"What is it now?" Brown asked.

Ace closed in upon the faint gleam until she reached out and plucked a small object from among the hummocky carpet of needles and low weeds. She turned it over and over in her fingers.

From everywhere and nowhere, a low musical trill warbled up and down the musical scale.

Brown scanned around, then zeroed in at Ace. The warble faded out. "What is *that?*"

"It's a cuff link."

Brown rubbed wet fingers on wet stubble. "I meant the singing sound, but — a cuff link? That makes no sense."

Ace lifted her gaze to Brown, golden eyes glinting. "Then what I say next will make it worse. I'm fairly sure it belongs to Bert."

Days earlier, the steady drone of a gasoline motor bored through the fog of Bert's unconsciousness. Numerous discomforts greeted his awakening. His head pounded like a kettledrum. A twist of cloth wedged between his jaws, cruel in its tension. It distorted the flesh of his lips and cheeks and mashed his tongue into his throat. Bodily aches mingled with a bone-deep chill, but his teeth could not chatter with cold because of the gag.

He opened his eyes, to no avail. A blindfold kept him in darkness. The running motor and sense of motion suggested that his crumpled body lay in a boat. A briny funk in his nostrils confirmed it. His first movements brought storms of pricking needles from returning circulation. Ropes bound his hands in front of him. The gag stifled his attempt to spew curses, and only strangled moans escaped his parched throat.

He squirmed to free his elbows, then clawed at the blindfold. With a woody clonk and a burst of pain, a rounded, hard object swatted his forearms away from his face.

A male voice growled, "Nicht!"

For a moment, Bert's mind flashed back in time. Cold, bare Great War prison cells hemmed him in. Bored interrogators with his blood on their brass knuckles sneered. The gloating face of the guard with the birthmark, Bert's special tormentor, hovered before his blinded eyes.

Where am I? What is happening?

Only seagulls answered his unspoken query.

The note of the motor's drone lowered in pitch. Water swished, and the motor cut altogether. Booted feet clomped on wood, but none of those unseen souls uttered a word. Bert struggled to hands and knees, fearing another blow.

Gravel scraped the boat's bottom. A man-sized splash sent flecks of water to Bert's face. Instead of a blow, hands fell upon his upper arms and lifted him to unsteady feet. Bert had no strength to resist as they dragged him over gunwales and into shallow waters. His chilled flesh barely felt the extra cold as he stumbled through icy wet.

One numb foot struck a rock, and Bert fell forward. His lurch evaded his captors' grip. By reflex, he extended his shackled hands and caught his fall, ending wrist-deep in gravel.

Mutters arose around him, then rough hands yanked at his blindfold before setting him back on his feet. He blinked as cloudy light flooded his eyes and blinked again at sight of his captors.

They numbered four, these apparitions of green and brown. Moss festooned their helmets, and smears of brown and green paint covered their pitiless faces. Similar decorations covered them from head to toe, and they barely resembled men in the end. They seemed mossy dead trees that shambled upon legs. They blended well with the dank forested shore. Even their rifles were painted in swampy themes, but the weapon outlines struck Bert as familiar. They were carbines from the Great War, of Ottoman design and German manufacture.

A clearing hugged the gravel shore, though trees crowned the hill upon which they had landed. Besides the bare motorboat in which they had arrived, no scrap of civilization could be seen. One swamp man gestured Bert upslope. He stumbled over mossy hummocks, but at least the exercise chased the numbness away. A grim smile grew upon his lips as he remembered his last stint as prisoner of war. They had escaped. They met Ace, and then they escaped.

Ace.

Bert's eyes narrowed. Ace and Quack and the rest, if anybody could find him, they could. He glanced down at his now shabby suit and the metal rings that imprisoned his hands. A glint of light from his cuff link set his fingers in motion. His eyes slid from swamp man to swamp man as his fingers worried his cuff link free.

Their intent eyes stared forward, though. Somehow, they had opened a black square in the ground. They marched into it, and Bert came along. But not before dropping his token.

Concrete steps led down into the earth, and a horrid smell assaulted Bert's nose. The stench was an evil mix of chemical factory and rot, and it made his eyes water. Haste drove the swamp men. They hustled him along until the steps leveled out.

One struck a match against the blackness. When metal bars appeared in the gloom, the rest of the soldiers pushed Bert into the cage. He fell with a crunch onto a carpet of dead beetles. With a watery clank, the swamp men tossed in a canteen. With a clang and a snick, they locked the cell door and fled as if devils nipped at their heels.

A boom from the exit echoed. Utter blackness descended, and complete silence.

The second boat got a less awkward reception. Proving they could learn from experience, the four associates lined up on the dock and observed. The second boat was smaller than the Hapennys', and the driver was dressed in a cozy fisherman's slicker. A dark mustache bristled from his upper lip, and he wasn't tall or broad-shouldered enough to be the Irishman they sought.

The associates helped tie up the small motorboat and held it steady for the man to disembark. He furrowed his forehead at them. They grinned.

"Well, thanks for the hand, friends. I'm Watts Langley. And who might you all be?" His voice was that of an orator, polished and controlled, with a Midwestern twang.

Tombstone was well-rehearsed. "Tombstone. Gooper. Quack. Sam. Pleasure, sir. Oh, and that's Abel and Bette Hapenny across the dock."

Watts waved across the dock, "Hello, there! You're a long way from home, aren't you?" He examined the soggy row of associates. "And where do you hail from? It's odd for Port Clam to get any visitors at all, and here we have six, all in the same day."

"Are you from Port Clam?" Quack said.

"No, no. I'm usually at the capitol, but from time to time, I make the rounds. So, where are you from, again?"

Sam said, "Sahibs! Sahibs! Yet another boat!"

Quack dodged bolting men for a second, delaying to grin big at Watts and say, "Talk later? We're here to meet a fellow."

Watts narrowed his eyes and watched them pelt down the dock to meet the new motorboat that approached. They lined up in a ragged row of diverse sizes and shapes.

The boat cruised in close.

Then its engine roared. Kicking up spray, the boat spun sharply and accelerated away.

The four whooped and shook their fists.

"Gallows!"

"Come back here, you coward!"

CHAPTER 12

Ace said, "I can't be absolutely sure, of course. But he owns cuff links identical to this."

She let Brown take the tiny ornamental item, silver inlaid with ebony. Ace hunched over and began padding in a spiral, intently examining the ground.

Brown joined in the scouting. "Footprints, you're thinking?"

"Yes. Anything."

Minutes passed.

"The rain is not helping."

"Nor the fading light."

The light rain softly hissed from all points of the compass, caressing their ears with timeless natural music.

Brown said, "We should push on. The sun will set soon, and Tillamook—"

Subtly, a footstep of Brown's resonated like a bass drum stuffed with batting. Ace whirled to see. He was halfway up one of the countless mossy mounds that made up the ground in the area.

Brown stepped again, more firmly.

Boom.

Ace stepped over and reached to rap with her knuckles on the tilted ground. Most of the taps echoed beneath their feet.

"Remarkable," Ace said. "It's a cellar door, like a tornado shelter or similar. It's metal but painted in

83

natural colors and decorated with moss and bracken. It's in plain sight and yet utterly invisible. Or nearly so. Now I can see some crushed grass from foot traffic. This line where they disappear must be one edge of the doors. Can you find handles? They must be here somewhere."

They traced the outlines of the tilted trapdoor by sense of touch. Wordlessly, they found the recessed handholds, and together they heaved the heavy double doors open.

They stood before the black rectangle of the entrance. Steep concrete stairs led down into the darkness.

Ace unslung her backpack and fished out the big radio and a pulse transmitter. She hid the pinger under the branch of a fern as the voice radio warmed up.

"*Sky Arrow One*, this is Ace," she said into the microphone. Brown took one step down into the bunker but hesitated to go further.

The radio fizzed with a tinny version of Gilbert's voice, "Copy, Ace. *Sky Arrow One* receiving. Over."

"Get a good triangulation on pulse transmitter three. It marks the location of some sort of underground facility. We're going in. Copy all that? Over."

"Copy. Over."

"Over and out."

Brown rubbed his hands together, trying to warm them. "The Mounties could use that radio. I never saw one so tiny before."

Ace jammed the radio back in her pack and joined Brown on the stairs down. "We'll need light. I have a few matches, but there's nothing dry out here to make a torch with. Let's go."

They descended. After a dozen steps, they were feeling their way as their eyes tried to adjust to the sudden darkness. The air was drier and silent.

Brown choked. "Eck! What is that stench?"

Ace sounded worried. "Decay? Decomposition? But, no, not really. There is a chemical tang to it, but it's not formaldehyde or ether."

Brown was silent as they inched their way deeper. The steps ended, and the floor flattened out. The floor was smooth and hard, but littered with stray pine needles and small crunchy objects that snapped under each footfall.

They inched forward, but the feeble light from the entrance illuminated nothing in front of them. Ace and Brown bumped into something cold and unyielding.

Brown felt with his hands. "Steel bars?"

His voice sounded dry. The room they were in must be cavernous.

Ace said, "I'll burn a match."

Shortly thereafter, a flare appeared between her hands.

Brown said, "Bars! Like a jail. There is an open door."

Thick steel pillars marched in rows, supporting a rusty steel roof. The concrete floor was strewn with dead beetles, and spiderwebs hung limply from the ceiling.

Ace's eyes searched to the right. Brown happened to be looking left. The match sputtered out.

Ace said, "I think it's wired for electric light." She strode over to what resembled a wall-mounted switch.

"No. Don't." Brown's voice shook.

"Why not?" Ace's fingers found the cold metal

switch and explored it in the darkness. It was a hefty industrial circuit breaker.

"I don't … I have a bad feeling about this place. Shapes. I saw … just a glimpse. We should leave."

Ace shuddered and frowned at the blob of slightly grayer darkness that was Douglas Brown. Her own feelings mirrored his, and she felt half smothered by shadows. "Can you be more specific?"

"Death," Brown said, his breath rapid and shallow. "Dead."

"Calm yourself. I'm going to try the switch. It's probably not connected, anyway."

But it was. Light from twenty bare bulbs flickered on, stretched out over the grid-like bunker, illuminating a scene far worse than Brown's imaginings.

CHAPTER 13

Sam, Quack, and Tombstone stood watching Gallows speed away, their fists clenched. Gooper glanced back at the boats belonging to Watts and the Hapennys. He buffeted Tombstone in the shoulder, who knocked into Quack, who knocked into Sam.

"Come on, lads!" Gooper cried. "Let's give chase!"

The Brit led the way along the dock in the Port Clam direction. He encountered Watts Langley first, as the gentleman was strolling by the Hapenny boat. "'Scuse us, guv." The bulky biologist fluffed his bushy red mustache into an upward curve. "Lend us your boat for a bit?"

"Out of the question." Langley straightened his back. "Out of the question." He glanced back at his small boat possessively, then eyed the four strangers with suspicion.

Gooper was barely deterred, if at all. "Cheers, mate. No worries!" He veered and lumbered toward the larger vessel where the Hapennys were tidying up. Letters proclaiming "*Violet*" marched across its stern.

Gooper put on his broadest grin. "What about it, Abel? Bette? Give Gallows a little excitement?"

Bette narrowed her eyes.

Abel said, "Well, our *Violet* is faster."

"True, true." Gooper wagged his head wisely. The three other associates milled behind him, dubious but willing.

Bette said sharply, "You gonna do something to him? Get him out of our hair, maybe?"

"Most assuredly, fine lady." Gooper puffed his chest out and crossed his meaty arms in slow motion. He winked conspiratorially. "If I get me way, a pretzel will envy the contortions I'll bend Gallows in."

Bette and Abel glanced at each other. Their eyebrows twitched.

The couple beamed at the quartet. Abel cried, "Cast off, crew! Let's catch us an Irishman! To the helm, Bette!"

The four leapt into action, untying the *Violet* as Abel started the motor.

"Lunatics," Watts Langley muttered. He turned his back pointedly and headed down the dock toward Port Clam.

The *Violet* followed the *Prince of Wales* westward, roughly the opposite direction of the lighthouse and the inland passage. The boats cruised a watery lane between forested hills. At first, the *Prince of Wales* cruised at a stroll, but when Gallows saw the *Violet* coming at full steam, he accelerated.

But the quarry's top speed was not impressive. Steadily, the *Violet* closed the distance. Abel gave a smug nod. "Told you. The *Violet's* faster."

Bette asked Tombstone, "What's with the rifle? Funny long-barreled rifle, at that."

"Well, it's fer shootin'."

Bette scowled. "Don't you sass me, cowboy."

Tombstone's mouth drooped. "I ain't sassin' ya, ma'am. It's my sharpshootin' rifle. Ace told me to be prepared for anything."

"Ace? Which one of you's Ace?"

"She ain't here. She's off tryin' t' find an Indian guide or somethin'."

"She?"

"Shore. Ace Carroway. Great War pilot."

"Oh, *that* Ace! So you really are chasing after a missing person. You told the truth! How 'bout that?"

Tombstone shrugged and spread his hands.

The lady barked a laugh. "Tellin' the truth's so rare, it's like tripping over a diamond."

"I agree with you there, ma'am. Bert's missin'. Gallows is our best lead."

"How come you know about the ghost liner?"

Tombstone shrugged. "People been mentioning it. Apparently, Bert saw it the night before he disappeared."

"Oh!" Bette took that news thoughtfully.

Abel asked, "What're you going to do when we catch up?"

Gooper answered instantly, "Vault the gap and storm aboard like buccaneers. Arrrr!"

Sam blinked. "Sahib? Truly? I'm uncertain that this piratical and energetic activity suits my," he patted his round tummy, "particular talents."

Gooper wiggled fuzzy red eyebrows at him. "You'll manage. You always do."

The chase wound left and right around tiny islands, the *Violet* coming closer and closer to the *Prince of Wales* all the time.

Quack said with intensity, "We're almost on top of him."

The two vessels split a pair of islands. The *Prince of Wales* ran through, its motor buzzing like giant wasp wings. Only yards behind, the *Violet* slowed as if it had run into a lake of molasses. A subtle hiss sound arose from below the hull. A few seconds later, the *Violet* ground to a dead stop.

Abel blurted, "Sandbar! Kill the engine!"

Bette shut off the engine. In the quiet, the buzz of the *Prince of Wales* trailed off in a cheeky diminuendo.

An hour later, the sun had set. With light fading, Gooper and Tombstone strained, up to their necks in water. They stood on a squishy, treacherous mud surface while their cheeks and splayed hands pressed against the prow of the *Violet*.

"C-c-cain't budge th' boat," Tombstone said through chattering teeth.

"Because *you* left your fancy — nay, ostentatious — boots aboard ship," Gooper said, also shivering profoundly.

"That's nonsense, ya fluffed-up hoot owl. No shoe in the world kin get a grip on this here muck."

"Eh, wot? It's like rugby in the rain, that's all."

But Gooper's words convinced no one, not even himself. In the end, the *Violet* stayed stuck, and they hauled their exhausted, dripping carcasses back on deck.

"T-T-Tombstone needs a blanket," Gooper said, though his own condition was equally dire.

Bette said, "Get under the wheelhouse, men. It's shelter, after a fashion. I already got the cookstove going. The chowder's gettin' hot, and one thing we do have is blankets."

Abel and Bette had screeched in fury when the ship first ran aground, but the next hour calmed them down. Now, they waxed philosophical about the situation.

Abel said, "We have rope enough to reach that rock sticking up back there. Well, I can't see it now. We'll have to wait until morning. You all can swim over and attach the line. Then some sideways pulls should drag us out, by and by."

Chowder was served.

Sam observed, "Lady and gentlemen. It has ceased to rain."

Quack said, "What brought you to Alaska, Abel, Bette?"

"We're terrible farmers," Abel said. "Hated Iowa."

"Got the wanderlust, anyway," Bette added.

"And I guess we're dreamers. Came to stake a claim, of course. Work hard for a few years and get rich. That was our plan."

From somewhere in her skirts, Bette pulled out an enormous Colt revolver. She broke it open and removed six shells, then began cleaning it.

Sam watched the operation with wide eyes.

Bette noticed. "Put your eyes back in their sockets, Sam. This is the West. How else does a body persuade a claim-jumper to keep on a-movin'?"

CHAPTER 14

In the sudden garish light of twenty bare bulbs, the contents of the underground bunker sprang into vivid relief. Bulky steel pillars supported a metal roof overhead. Poured concrete formed the floor. The soulless architecture might have been conceived as a warehouse, perhaps, but now it housed only death.

Ace's and Brown's eyes riveted to the ragged rows of corpses that covered the floor. The desiccated bodies contorted in positions of agony. Hands curled in claw shapes. Open mouths gaped as if gasping for air with tongues shriveled inside. Mercifully, eye sockets showed only as shadowy pits. Most of the bodies wore grayed and partially decomposed clothing.

Purpose was evident. Lanes of bare floor allowed access to the rows of cadavers. They were not in piles but jammed together in a single layer, feet pointed one way and heads pointed the other. The shabby space held only human remains and the barest of furnishings. Along the near wall marched jail-style cages, all empty. Over in one corner, two corpses rested upon two tables, but these bodies were incomplete. The threadbare sheets that covered them could not disguise that they lacked heads.

Brown weaved on his feet and emitted choked sounds of incomprehension. He bolted toward the stairs out, stumbling over his own feet. Ace's mouth dropped open in a rictus of horror. As Brown's clattering feet receded, she recited, "Within me is a center of peace that cannot be disturbed. Be still and look within. Within, there is no attachment. Within, there is no fear. Within, there is no urgency. Look within and know peace."

In the end, her Wing Chun mantra overrode her instinctive reaction to the monstrous scene. Her pulse slowed to match her controlled breathing. She shook her clenched fists until they flopped into relaxed hands. "To work, Ace."

A few minutes later, Brown returned. Pale and wobbly-kneed, he nevertheless bore a determined clench to his jaw. He found Ace bending over a nearby corpse and almost reversed course. He cleared his tight throat.

Ace swept a glance up and down him. She kept her remarks carefully clinical. "At least seventy-five bodies, all male."

Brown's jaw muscles worked. "It's a macabre nightmare."

"Most are dressed in the same uniform, that of the Canadian infantry, or so I suspect. Can you confirm my guess by looking at the insignia? But this one is a sailor, not a soldier."

He forced himself to focus on the threadbare indications of rank. Woodenly, he responded. "Yes, Canadian infantry from the Great War. Is it the crew of the *Sir John Thompson* and the troops it carried?"

Ace stood. She placed each foot deliberately as she visited the tables upon which the headless corpses lay.

Brown about-faced, his skin paling a shade whiter.

Ace's voice seemed strained and muffled. "It seems likely. I haven't seen absolute proof so far."

"Then it's a massacre." Brown kept his back to the decapitated mummies and what Ace might be doing with them. He regarded therefore the empty jail cells. All their doors stood ajar. A silvery scrawl on the rough concrete wall attracted his attention, and he went inside and knelt.

He squinted, then called, "Do the letters H-E-D-C-B-I-I-I mean anything to you?"

In an eyeblink, Ace whisked over and hovered behind him. Her voice, though soft, vibrated with emotion. "In a word, yes! That stands for Hubert Ewing Devery Christopher Bostock the third."

"I see drops of blood. Here and here."

"Injured," Ace said, "is vastly different than dead. Frankly, I'm elated." And she sounded it. Her face lost its grim aspect, and her spine straightened.

Brown flicked some beetle shells aside to pluck a tiny metallic object from the floor. He held it up for Ace. "His other cuff link, or what's left of it. He used it to mark his initials and three hash marks below. I guess it means he was caged here for three days."

"Oh." Ace's widened eyes speared to regard the rows of corpses, and she shuddered.

Sympathetic pain laced Brown's voice. "Poor fellow. Poor, poor fellow."

More accurately, Bert had slept three times. In the absence of any kind of light, his rhythm of sleep was his only clock, crude though it was. The arrival of bread and water interrupted his second sleep. Match flares lit this visit, too. Again, the pair of swamp men tripped over themselves to get away once their duty was done.

Bert scratched marks on the wall after his third sleep. His head had stopped aching from Gallows's wallop, but a new, sinister throb arose from long exposure to the ghastly atmosphere. Bert could feel his strength draining away. The short rations surely caused part of his fatigue, but the poisonous funk in the air dragged at him more.

Dreams blended with hallucinations. A few pleasant visions unfolded before his blinded eyes, but most of his deliriums writhed and twisted with nauseous discomfort. He relived the moment the Ottoman guard with the birthmark over his eye shot him in the shoulder. He refought Ottoman aeronauts and pressed his thumbs again on Quack's wounded thigh to staunch the rapid flow of blood. Quack mumbled about walking the sky trails, preparing himself for death. Almost peacefully, Bert's friend prepared himself for life's end.

"Don't go, Quack. Warburton. Don't leave."

With a jolt, Bert awakened.

"Quack," he said to the dead air, "you lived, buddy. It came out all right."

He dragged himself to his feet, and his head swam. A note of desperation colored his speech. "And Ace removed the bullet from my shoulder, remember? And we won the war. And that guard died, just last year, wasn't it? I bet nobody mourned him, the cowardly rat."

Bert huffed tainted air, but it only brought him a fresh wave of dizziness. In the darkness, Ace's face formed. Not beautiful and certainly not symmetric, but electric with vibrant life. Even the scars that raked across the side of her face seemed to accentuate a vivid, immediate sense of presence.

"So help me if I get out of here, I'm going to wear Ace down. We can at least go to dinner and a movie. Without Quack getting in the way."

An image of Quack replaced that of Ace in Bert's fevered imaginings. Among countless other irritants, the debonair actor competed with Bert for attention from women. But trading insults with the man kept Bert's wits sharp. Not to mention the unspoken code. If one could save the other by intercepting a bullet, without a second thought the sacrifice would be made.

With a bang and a rattle, he pounded a palm on a cold steel bar. "Where *am* I? What *is* this foul pit I'm stewing in? Come on, Ace. Come on, Quack. You can find me. It could happen any minute."

As if on cue, a boom rang out. The exterior doors had flung open once again. This time, wan light streamed in. Bert blinked.

A slim silhouette descended the stairs, breaking the distant daylight into rays of shadow. "Ace?"

But Bert's hopes soon shattered. The outlined figure possessed too many sharp angles, and it lacked Ace's catlike gait.

A baritone voice drawled, "Still there, Mr. Bostock?"

Bert knew he should recognize that voice, but his wooly head couldn't put a name to the easy baritone.

"Mr. Bostock?" The figure reached to the wall to grip an electrical relay. With a spark and a bang, light overwhelmed Bert's atrophied vision.

But when he could see again, nothing that came into focus was welcome. Not a single, horrible thing.

Chapter 15

Brown and Ace extinguished the lights and climbed out of the charnel house, their footfalls solemn. Without speaking, they closed the doors and pumped clean air into their lungs.

"Huh," Brown said. "The rain stopped."

"Good. Perhaps we'll see stars to navigate by. Come on. Tillamook is out here, somewhere. We'll need a little luck in finding her."

"I'll say."

"Why is she 'the outcast,' Brown?"

"No idea. She left her people, and that is all I know. Unlike most folks, she knows how to keep silent."

"She lives in isolation. Is she a loner by nature?"

"No," Brown stated flatly. His eyebrows worked, and his next words were less certain. "I mean, I don't think so. I was only with her for a day or two. She's an interesting person."

Ace recovered her pulse transmitter. After a few minutes of hiking, she flexed her shoulders and straightened her back. Her face remained solemn, but the tension released, and the shadows that had plagued her seemed absent. Once they were under cover of trees, she checked in with *Sky Arrow One*. The pulse transmitter had been duly triangulated and mapped, Gilbert reported. Ace didn't tell him what was *there*.

After the radio call, Ace and Brown trudged parallel to the glistening water lane in the fading twilight. Trees closed in on them once again, but the glimpses of water and the slope of the land kept their course straight.

Free of the oppression of the body bunker, Ace allowed herself a deep breath and a sighing exhale.

Brown said, "Remember when you said we'd be lucky to find Tillamook? I'm surprised the word 'luck' escaped your lips, Miss Carroway. I've never met a head as cool as yours. Surely you don't believe in luck."

"Cool? I'm starting to think I'm misunderstood that way. Don't think I wasn't a hair's breadth away from screaming and running."

"I don't believe it. You went to examine those … ones with no heads."

"I'm a doctor."

"I thought you were a pilot."

"Yes, well, that, too. But I wondered why they had been decapitated. My guess is that someone performed a clumsy autopsy on them. You couldn't see, but I found skulls, bisected. The heads were removed, put in a vice, and sawed open. That would give ready access to the brain matter."

"Augh! Stop!"

"Yes, all right. But from precise observations, we can deduce better facts. The autopsy was systematic and calculated, done in cold blood, for one. For another, it wasn't professional. No trained surgeon or coroner guided the operation. For a third, to bother to do any sort of autopsy implies an interest in the connection between the cause of death and the effects on — certain major organs."

"They weren't shot?"

"No, Mr. Brown."

"I guess I just assumed. Well, then, how did they

die?"

Ace did not answer. As twilight became night, the darkness blurred her burnished features. Brown saw little hope of reading emotions there. He said, "Well?"

"I have a guess, but I don't want to cause you more indigestion."

"I can take it. We're out in the fresh air now. Not in that ... mass grave."

"I believe they were killed with poison gas."

Brown's steps faltered. "Egad! Why do you say gas?"

"A few things. The smell, for one. No marks on the bodies. The contorted positions. The lack of *living* spiders or beetles. Also, the bars of the cells were imports of Ottoman manufacture."

"Ottoman? How do you know that?"

Ace spat bitter words. "Past experience."

"Oh, right. I forgot you were a veteran."

"Gas might explain the need to autopsy, as well, if the Ottomans wanted to investigate the medical effects of gas on the victims' tissues."

"Augh. That's grotesque. But I asked. I got what I asked for."

They trudged on for a few more minutes.

Brown said, "Suddenly, I'm relieved."

"Why?"

"If all the troops were back in that bunker, there won't be any bodies on the *Sir John Thompson* itself."

"That's logical."

Brown shook himself. "Whether they died on the ship or later on, their ghosts haunt that mass crypt. I've never felt such dread."

A strangled growl emerged from Ace's throat,

caught between agreement and denial.

"Oh," Brown said. "You don't believe in ghosts."

"I do, metaphorically." Ace sounded reflective. "The violence of the Great War lives on. The lives cut short, the shattered trust, the new ways of killing. Such manifestations of our darker sides echo and re-echo. These concepts are invisible. But, still, they are real. They are the ghosts of the Great War."

Brown rubbed his chin for a while. Then he patted his belly. "Can we stop for nuts and jerky?"

A new voice sounded from between the dark trees. "Nuts and jerky? Share, please!" The voice was female and contained a note of laughter.

"Tillamook!"

The voice said, "Maybe, maybe. But who walks with this hungry man?"

"I'm Ace Carroway," the scarred pilot said. "I'm searching for a friend who went missing four days ago. His disappearance connects with Mr. Brown's mystery, so he and I are working together."

The voice said, "Ace Carroway. Well, all right. As long as you also have nuts and jerky. I'm starved."

Brown said, with a pang of concern, "Are you?" He shucked off his backpack and rummaged.

A dim shape separated from the trees and padded near. "No, not truly starving. Just hungry."

Less hastily than Brown, Ace shed her backpack, too, and quaffed water from her canteen. "I'm glad you found us, Tillamook. We had only rudimentary directions."

Tillamook snatched a hunk of jerky offered by Brown and tore into it. The darkness obscured her deerskin clothes, but she seemed of medium height and build. Between chews, she said, "Ace Carroway likes big words."

"Tillamook," Brown said. "We need your help. We just saw the most horrible thing: a room full of dead bodies. Probably the crew of the *Sir John Thompson*. Been there for years."

Around her chipmunked cheeks, Tillamook said, "Why do you need my help? Bury them yourself."

Brown forced a chuckle. "I don't want to go anywhere near there again. But we still don't know what's going on. We need to dive at the *Sir John Thompson*."

Ace added, "And we need to find Bert. We also need to sort out who the men with guns are and if they are the same as Arni's swamp men that come for supplies at night."

Tillamook swallowed. "Well, that's quite a list."

Chapter 16

Tombstone and Gooper stopped shivering after ravenously inhaling Bette's soup. They heaped praise upon her cooking until she giggled. They and the others tucked themselves into various corners of the *Violet* and attempted to catch some sleep. Only Sam relaxed into a limp pose of closed eyes and deep, blissful breathing. The rest found the chilly temperatures and unyielding wood of the hull too uncomfortable for slumber.

The moon rose above banks of fog, illuminating the vaporous shapes in hues of silver.

Faint and dreamlike at first, eerie whistles and sweeping glissandos diffused from the sea into the air. Sets of clicks like the opening of a balky hinge added to the haunting symphony.

Quack was the first to sit up. "What *is* that?"

Fabric rustled loud in the quiet night as others sat or stood. Then everyone froze as a long, chilling tone slid from soaring treble heights to a mid-tone tremolo. Only slumbering Sam escaped the prickling of goosebumps forming on skin chilled, not by temperature, but by fear.

The eerie concert continued, slowly growing louder. Abel seized the arm of his wife with one hand and pointed outward to the waters with his other. He rasped, "Look!"

Bette's gaze followed the pointing finger, and she

inhaled sharply. "There it is!"

The ghost liner glided through the mists into full view. Its portholes glowed a faint yellow. Its pale hull bore no insignia. The waters around it subtly glistened and writhed. The otherworldly tapestry of tones and clicks continued.

Nothing moved on deck, but a human figure, perhaps a statue, stood wedged in the prow. One trouser leg and one boot stuck out from under its bulky coat. The vague impression of a bearded face lurked in the shadow of its fisherman's hat.

The figure remained immobile as the luxurious vessel cruised past. A petite bow wave parted before it like a foamy mustache. It steered well clear of the sandbar in a long arc, receding down a dimly lit waterway between islands.

Its odd polyphonic song faded, too, until the stern disappeared into a fogbank.

"It's real," Abel whispered.

"We'll be rich." Bette's moonlit face grew dreamy. She leaned against Abel, cheek to shoulder.

Gooper's pale forehead wrinkled up. "That's wot Bert saw?"

Quack replied, low and grim, "Yes. And he disappeared scant hours later."

Tillamook led Ace and Brown, weaving through drenched trees and soggy shrubbery. "Last time I helped you, copper man[3], I lost a boat and almost got filled with bullets."

Brown said, "I'll pay for the boat!"

"So you said." Tillamook's voice grew lower and more thoughtful. "I didn't think you meant it."

"Well, I did. And I do. Tillamook? Where are we going?"

"It's late. I'll take you to my camp. I have some very comfortable patches of dirt to sleep on. Premium real estate." Notes of laughter burbled beneath her words.

Tillamook led them to a spot on the shore. The moon was up now. It was at gibbous phase, waning but bright enough to sculpt the fogbanks into fantastic silver beasts dancing like slow-motion acrobats.

"That's my canoe." Their guide pointed to a long shadow by a downed, waterlogged tree that sloped into the lazy waves. "It can carry two, so that means two trips. My camp is across the water."

The moonlight fell on Tillamook's sturdy, pleasant face. Lines of good humor crinkled the outside corners of her eyes. A slender beaded headband stretched across her brow, under which hair parted into two braids. Her sharp eyes roved, quick to challenge and never deferential, full of insolence but also sparkling with humor.

Tillamook caught Ace looking and stared back, hard. Silence stretched until half of Ace's face lifted in a lopsided smile. Tillamook pursed her lips and gave the tiniest of nods. "I'll take the copper man first."

---

[3] Tillamook's free associations can be hard to follow. In this case, a Canadian Mountie is a sort of police officer, and police wear copper badges.

Ace inclined her head. "Of course."

Shortly, the guide and Mountie arranged themselves in the petite cedar craft. Ace helped them launch, and they paddled away without a word spoken. They headed for a knob of land a few hundred yards away. The twisted shapes of the fjords made it impossible to know for sure if the forested lump was an island or a peninsula. The labyrinthine waterways kept their secrets well.

Ace took the opportunity provided by solitude to answer the call of nature, then plopped down by the water and munched on nuts. Her lips curved upward. "I wonder if there's a little chemistry between Tillamook and Brown. If so, what's she asking him right now?"

When she ceased chewing, her ears caught the hints of a high-pitched whistle, tickling at the edge of audibility. She controlled her breathing and entered a silent Wing Chun meditation. Her eyes closed.

A similar whistle sounded, louder. Mysterious staccato ticks spoke. Ace rose to her feet. The avant-garde performance poised between music and noise. As time passed, it grew more distinct but never louder than a whisper.

The tickle of a presence to her left made Ace's eyes fly open. They widened, and she sucked in a sharp breath. In a stately promenade, a spectral yacht glided down the channel. Its yellow portholes shone like the eyes of a malevolent spider. Quiet splashes from its bow wave mingled with the whistles and scoops of the unnerving accompaniment. There was no other sound. No screw, no motor, no burning fuel. No trail of smoke rose from its angled stack. A one-legged man, ornament or captain, stood unmoving in the prow, watching with two pinpricks for eyes.

Ace's brow wrinkled.

It stayed wrinkled after the glide of the liner carried it around Tillamook's island and the uncanny sonic accompaniment died away.

CHAPTER 17

Tillamook returned to find Ace retracting the antenna on her portable radio. The pilot stuffed the device into her pack and tossed the pack into the canoe. She boarded, too, taking up a paddle.

"Did you see the ghost liner?" Ace said to Tillamook's back.

"Yes, yes."

"Ah? You've seen it before?"

But Tillamook paddled and said no further word. At the far shore, in silence, they pulled the canoe up into the trees. A few dozen yards further upslope, the land dimpled. In this sheltered bowl, Brown awaited them. A firepit sat in front of a lean-to composed of sticks and strips of bark, and those two features comprised the entirety of the camp.

"I saved some tinder," Tillamook said. "Make yourselves at home." She busied herself at the firepit, scooping dirt and ash to the sides with a hunk of bark. In moments, she uncovered the coals of her previous fire. She fed the coals twigs and blew air to tease open flames back to life.

Brown and Ace gratefully dropped their packs on the moist earth. The buckskin-clad Mountie folded his legs and plopped down. "That was uncanny."

Ace said, "The ghost liner?"

"Yes! Those eerie squeaks and groans, but no engine noise. Was that one-legged man a statue? He

111

looked real."

"I have to admit." Ace flashed a grin. "The prospect of a silent engine has my mind awhirl with ideas. No idea that goes anywhere, though. I can't fathom it."

Brown blew air from his nostrils. "Maybe it was in our minds. Or it really was from the spirit world."

"No," Ace blurted. "It didn't feel like the — like earlier today."

Brown lifted an eyebrow at the shaky note in her voice. Tillamook glanced up from her work for a moment, then went back to coaxing a flame to grow.

Ace cleared her throat. "Do you need firewood, Tillamook?"

The native woman sent Ace a guarded glance. "Sure. I always seem to. Wood you pick up will be wet tonight, so the fire will be steamy."

"I'll choose as best I can." Ace sidled toward the edge of the dell to scavenge for sticks that might not be completely waterlogged.

Brown stayed put. "We still want to dive at the *Sir John Thompson*. Can you take us there?"

Tillamook said, "Tomorrow, yes. Brown man, you look sleepy."

Brown clapped a hand over a yawn. "You're right."

"You two can sleep. I will take first watch," Tillamook said.

No one argued. After the fire was stoked, Brown and Ace nested next to it.

Brown held out his pistol to Tillamook. "Here, take this. It shoots poison darts, so it's not very long range."

"Will it stop a bear?"

"Probably," Brown said.

"I'd say a definite yes," Ace said, rubbing her shoulder.

Tillamook's eyes flicked from one to the other. "You shot her?"

Brown barked a soft laugh. "Yeah."

An impish little smile spread over Tillamook's features.

Ace smiled a little in return. She closed her eyes and shortly knew only dreams.

Until a sharp bang jolted her awake. As if stung, she rolled away from the fire and landed in a crouch. Instinctively, she quested this way and that until she spotted the dim outline of Tillamook and a second figure. Tillamook held the gun but did not fire a second shot. The other figure, tall and male, staggered. Like a Shakespearian actor milking a death scene, he tottered for long moments before falling to his knees. In slow motion, he tipped forward and fell on his face.

Brown thrashed as he lay by the fire, coming awake with a struggle. He sat up and rubbed his eyes. "What was that?"

"That was fun!" Tillamook said. "I mean, it would be bad if I killed him, but just shooting him was a kick! Wait. What kind of poison? Will he die?"

Ace padded over and heaved the man over. "The poison is curare, and he will not die unless overdosed. Then, the muscles with which he breathes will relax, and he will suffocate." She plucked a dart from between the man's ribs.

Brown found his feet and stepped forward to peer into his guide's face. "By heaven! Tillamook, are you all right?"

"Fine, fine. You worry a lot, copper man."

They all three stared down at the limp fellow staring up at them. His eyes tracked them, but his mouth drooped slack and his limbs were all but boneless.

Brown's eyes widened. "Wait, I know him! That's—"

Ace finished for him. "Gallows. His full name might be Oren O'Gallagher. But it might not. He's an experienced liar. Let's drag him to the fire."

Brown and Ace each took an armpit and dragged the fellow over. Ace searched his pockets. She ignored his money but removed a belt knife. She also removed a deck of playing cards and examined its box. "Can you talk, Gallows?"

His eyes pled and widened with fear. Ace narrowed her own and clapped a pair of fingers to Gallows's neck. His face darkened, and an abnormal stillness lay upon his chest and belly.

Ace crisply announced, "He's not breathing."

Tillamook and Brown grew quizzical expressions, as if searching for a joke in Ace's short sentence.

Ace knelt and tilted Gallows's head back. "Brown, take his shoes off and chafe his feet." She sealed her lips to his and puffed air.

Brown said, "What? Oh, heavens!" He fumbled at Gallows's boots.

Tillamook said, "Whoa. She's kissing him."

Gallows's sweater-clad chest inflated. Ace raised her head and watched his chest fall again, air streaming out of his mouth. She muttered, "Tillamook. Gracious. I'm trying to save his life here." When his air stopped streaming, Ace sealed her mouth to his and puffed again.

Brown managed to get his boots off and began briskly rubbing the paralyzed man's feet. "Like this?" he asked.

Tillamook's eyebrows arched high. "This is going to make a great story later."

Ace said, between applications of artificial respiration, "Yes, like that. It will draw blood to his feet and dilute the curare. Tillamook, do the same to his hands and wrists."

A few long minutes later, Gallows resumed breathing. Ace rocked back on her heels, watched his chest rise and fall, and allowed herself a muted smile of triumph.

Tillamook said, "We're done?"

Brown said, "We're done. He didn't die."

Ace leaned over Gallows. "But I'll kill you yet if you don't start telling me the truth. The *whole* truth, got it?"

Ace didn't wait for an answer. She fetched her canteen and gave herself a drink. Then she trickled water down Gallows's throat.

He swallowed and coughed. Weakly, he wheezed, "Begorra!"

Brown frowned at Ace. "Should we tie him up before he regains control of himself?"

Tillamook added, "Why is he here? He is not one of the gunmen, is he?"

Ace laid her canteen down and picked up Gallows's deck of cards, unboxing them. "No need for tying, not in his state. And, no, he's not one of the gunmen. He's here to attempt to pillage the ghost liner."

Tillamook's sunny face darkened. "No."

Ace sorted Gallows's cards. She raised an eyebrow at Tillamook.

Brown also looked askance at Tillamook.

Tillamook raised her chin. "No. Stop him."

Brown said, "Why? What do you know, Tillamook?"

Tillamook snorted. "I know that he, or you, should not bother with this ghost liner. Don't ask me more."

Ace chewed on her lower lip. "It would help us evaluate the situation."

Brown nodded fervently. "Please?"

"No." Tillamook's head tilted to one side. "Well, one more hint. You'll just cause heartbreak. And there's no glory in it."

"That's," Brown said, "not very specific."

"Who cares? Stop this one." Tillamook gave Gallows a dig in the ribs with her booted foot.

Gallows muttered, "I'm a bloody gobshite. Never knew such a headache. Ye should'ha let me die."

Ace said, "Time to interview Gallows, I think. Turn your head this way, Gallows." Ace bent down and physically moved Gallows's head so that Ace hovered in his field of view.

"Lass. Improved my view, that did."

Ace's teeth closed tight, and her jaw muscles rippled. "You'd do better to speak only when spoken to, Gallows."

"I'm terrible. I know. For every kiss I win, I endure ten slaps on the cheek."

"Gallows, you *are* terrible." Ace fanned out some of his own cards for him to see. "Most decks of cards only have *one* ace of spades. Somehow, yours has three."

"You know, those are my private, personal things, lass."

Ace tossed the cards in the direction of the fire. They fluttered, and some landed in the flames, where they began to curl and blacken.

"I'm changing my mind," Tillamook said. "I'm starting to like her."

Brown grimaced. "She has a certain unstoppable freight train sort of charm."

Ace curled a hand into Gallows's artfully cabled sweater front and leaned in close. "Gallows, I don't enjoy abusing a helpless man, so here's your watershed moment. Tell me everything you know about Bert. *Now.*"

Gallows's pupils flared wide. He studied Ace's resolute jawline. "All right, I'll come clean, but be advised that I have more than one confession."

Ace released his sweater. "Confess away."

"I'll confess it. I think I'm in love." Gallows managed a numb-lipped smile.

Ace curled her fingers into Gallows's sweater again, her expression tightening.

"As for Bert, aye. I plead guilty. I needed some cash, and the Bostonian was rich as Croesus. I knocked him on the head and took his money. Too bad. Likeable fellow. But he got less a headache than I've got right now, I'll wager."

Ace's expression didn't relax. "Then what? You just left him?"

"Ah, not quite, something a little strange. A gent named Watts Langley happened by. He's with the territorial government."

"Yes. Go on." Ace planted fists on her hips.

"Well, he kindly offered to *not* have me locked up if I would … walk away."

"And you walked."

"Aye. But, lass, seeing the look of disappointment in your eye, well, I'll never do it again."

"I really hate you, Gallows."

"I have something more to say. Indulge me?"

"What is it?"

"The next few days, I bought a little boat and some supplies, but I also went to the government house and applied my charm. Which charm, by the way, works on everyone except you." Gallows favored Ace with a hopeful little smile.

Ace's mouth remained a compressed flat line.

The Irishman sighed. "Where was I? Oh, yes. Charm. I charmed a librarianish woman in the governor's office. I asked her about Watts Langley and his job and the like."

"All right, I'm interested. What did you find out?"

"He's titled the Territorial Inspector. He answers to nobody except the governor. The articles that created the office don't list any duties."

Ace waved both her hands. "Wait, wait, wait. The Territorial Inspector's office?"

"Aye, that's the name. Why? You look like you've seen a ghost."

"Not a ghost, but the Territorial Inspector's office bought all of Morgan Mining's smelted titanium."

Gallows blinked in incomprehension. "Titanium?"

Ace gave a single, emphatic nod. "I assumed the company foreman had misspoken the name of the agency that purchased the metal, but it seems he hadn't." She let go of his sweater and shook a finger at him. "We're off track. Tell me more about what you found out."

"Aye, but there's not a lot more to tell. The office was created four or five years back."

Ace's head tilted to one side. "Perhaps by Adam S. Kleine, the suicide governor?"

Gallows's mouth dropped open in amazement, but he snapped it shut a moment later. "Correct, lass. And the office budget is a whopper. A thousand dollars a year. Spent on what, the librarian could not say. Whatever it is, it's not charity work."

"I should say not." Ace's eyes glinted in the firelight. "Abducting unconscious Bostonians isn't exactly the same moral level as feeding orphans."

Chapter 18

For the temporary crew of the *Violet*, morning brought a swim in the frigid Alaskan waters. Tombstone grumbled, "I ain't dried out from yesterday yet. I ain't warmed up, neither."

Lack of comfort notwithstanding, all four helped string a rope to a rock outcrop. They heaved and tugged in seven wrong ways before settling on a method. They stretched the rope tight. Crawling hand over hand to the midpoint, they all gripped the rope and bounced in unison. After gaining some slack, they tightened the rope and yanked again. In a series of six-inch victories, they dragged the *Violet* off the sandbar.

Arms trembling from overuse and teeth chattering from deathly chill, the four associates dragged themselves back aboard.

The Hapennys were pleased with the ghost liner sighting and therefore philosophical about having gotten stuck. Furthermore, the Carroway associates did all the work of unsticking. But the Hapennys' pleasure did not extend so far as to continue the relationship with the four men. As fast as the *Violet* could go, Abel and Bette raced to Port Clam. They deposited the men at the dock and sped away, back into the fjords and islands to search for evidence of the ghost liner.

Though their packs and equipment were dry and warm, the men themselves resembled half-frozen, half-drowned cats.

"S-S-Sahibs, I do not think my legs will carry me as

far as the dirigible."

Sky Arrow One could not be seen. The hill it sat upon poked up into low clouds, and its crest was obscured.

Tombstone said, "Don't worry none, Sam. We need to get warm, and pronto, or we'll all catch pneumonia."

Stiffly, they lurched down the dock toward Hulda's trading post. Watts Langley's boat was there, but not Gallows's.

Quack said, "Look. There's a badge on that boat. 'Official — Alaskan Territorial Government,' it says."

"Good ter know, mate," Gooper said. "Just in case we need some bureaucratic obstruction."

"That's awful pessimistic of you, Gooper," Tombstone said. "Good on you. You're comin' 'round to the right way of looking at life."

"There's no such thing as a sunny side right now, lizard breath. Oi'll never be warm again. Never."

No one contradicted him.

They bumbled through the trading post door. Watts Langley in a bow tie and a thickset man of about forty years sat in chairs near the stove. A kettle bubbled atop the wood-fired stove, and the smell of coffee wafted in the air.

"G-g-greetings, gentlemen," Sam said.

The four surrounded the stove like hummingbirds drinking nectar. With stiff fingers, Quack opened the firebox and stuffed three more sticks of firewood inside.

Langley wore a smirk. "Back from the chase, I see. How did it go?"

Tombstone scowled and held his hands toward the

stove. "How does it look like it went?"

"Did the Hapennys throw you overboard?"

Quack elbowed Tombstone in the ribs and answered, "No, no. We got stuck on a sandbar overnight. We lost Gallows, of course. We pulled free this morning after at least an hour in the drink."

The older man spoke up. A fluffy plaid blanket (at which the four associates cast envious glances) lay across his lap. Fuzzy brown eyebrows danced when he spoke with a light, vaguely European lilt. "Who are the Hapennys? Who is Gallows? And who are you?"

Quack said, "I'm Quack." He gestured at his companions. "Tombstone. Sam. Gooper. We're friends of Bert Bostock, who's gone missing."

Langley said, "Wait. Bert? Not the passenger on the *Kodiak Minnow*?"

"The same," Quack said. "You're on our interview list, too, Mr. Langley. You're one of the last to see him before he disappeared. It's just that chasing Gallows seemed more urgent."

Gooper rumbled, "Lyin' Irishman."

Langley scrunched his brows together. "Well, I didn't know he'd gone missing. We all became chums during the trip. It stretched days longer because of engine trouble, you see. But we all went our separate ways in Juneau." Langley smoothed his mustache. "But tell me, if he went missing in Juneau, why in the world are you in Port Clam?"

Gooper took over. "Gallows, o'course. We caught th' rummy blighter lyin', is why. Nothin' overt. Wee little lies. Shows 'e's hidin' summat."

"So Gallows came here. I wonder why?" Langley beetled his brows and began chewing on his lower lip.

"Who's Gallows?" repeated the man with the bushy eyebrows.

Langley gestured to the fellow. "This is Oskar, by the way. He repairs boats for the locals. Oskar, I only know Gallows from the trip north on the *Kodiak Minnow*. Never met him before that. He's Irish and likes to tell tall tales. That's all I know."

Gooper inhaled until Quack threw an elbow into his ribs. Gooper subsided, and Quack said, "He's an opportunist, I guess you'd say. He's down here hunting for the ghost liner, like the Hapennys."

Oskar's eyes bugged out. "Ghost liner?"

Sam said, "A local legend. You do not know about it, sahib?"

Oskar shifted his weight and sat straighter. "Didn't say I didn't hear about it. I'm surprised word got all the way to Juneau, that's all."

Langley wave a nonchalant hand in the air. "We'll simply have to dispel such nonsense. There's no such thing."

"Oh, but there is," Sam said. "All my companions saw it last night. Alas, I slept through the event, and my friends did not think to wake me." Sam shot accusatory glances at his fellow associates.

"But there's no such thing!" Langley hissed.

Quack wore a quiet, ironic smile. "There wasn't much gold in Juneau, either, but that didn't stop a gold rush."

Langley's face grew redder. "Blast. Blast and double blast. We don't want a bunch of *pirates* invading Port Clam!"

"They will go away when they don't find anything," Oskar said. In contrast to Langley, Oskar wasn't livid with rage. If anything, he had paled.

Sam's eyes watched the pair intently, and a line furrowed between his black eyebrows.

Gooper sighed in happy obliviousness. "Me clothing's startin' ter steam. I'm in 'eaven."

Langley said, his flush fading, "You should give Hulda two bits for the extra wood."

"Oh, most certainly, sir, at the very least," Sam said.

Langley studied the quartet huddled by the stove. His eyes narrowed. "Where's your boat? I didn't see it tied up at the dock."

Quack smirked. "We flew. By airship."

Langley frowned. "Don't joke with me. I hate that."

Quack's expression drooped. Gooper rushed to his rescue. "Langley, Quack 'ere's no joker. 'E's as level as a carpenter's bench. Didn't yew see the bloody great airship parked on the big hill?" Gooper poked a thumb in the direction of the fog-wrapped ridge.

Langley's face began closing down, transforming to an icy, unfeeling mask.

Gooper continued, "'Ooever kidnapped Bert, if that's wot 'appened, should've picked on a bloke with fewer friends, tell yew wot."

Langley, now with perfect composure, stood and daintily smoothed the fabric covering his thighs. "Well, it was a pleasure meeting all of you. My business takes me elsewhere now. Do enjoy Port Clam while you are here, and the, you know, fish. Or trees. Whatever the attraction is."

Langley didn't wave. He pivoted on his heel and stalked out the door. All eyes watched.

CHAPTER 19

While Gallows deeply slept, Brown tied the rogue's ankle to a tree.

In the morning, Ace performed her daily exercise ritual behind a tree near Tillamook's camp. The slight relocation avoided the inevitable stares and comments Ace's grueling routine would surely cause. She prided herself on being immune from embarrassment. But, still, being away from Gallows seemed preferable to being within view.

Without intending to, Ace overheard Brown and Tillamook talking. Tillamook said, "You've been acting funny since you came, Chack[4]."

"Have I?" Brown said. "Well, maybe it was all the dead bodies."

"No. The way you look at me. Speak to me."

"Oh. *That.*"

"Yes. That."

Any hard edges to Brown's voice softened. "Away from you, in Juneau and Victoria … well, it felt wrong. I felt wrong."

"Chack. Stop. I am the runaway, remember? The deserter. I am dead to my people and a stranger in the world."

Brown said, "I will stop my mouth, if you ask. But I cannot stop my eyes."

"You are a bastard."

---

[4] Chinook jargon: eagle.

Gallows's sleep-slurred voice interposed, "You *are* a bastard. Did you tie me up?"

"Of course. So would you, if you were us."

"Aye. Excellent point, that."

Ace skidded down the sides of the dell to the camp, covered in sweat. She headed straight for her canteen for a deep drink.

Gallows sighed at the sight. "All of a sudden, despite all my sufferings, my mood lifts."

Tillamook banked the fire, burying the coals for possible future use. She glanced at Ace. "There you are," she accused.

Brown said, "We're ready to head for the *Sir John Thompson*."

Ace lowered her canteen and wiped her lips with the back of a sinewy hand. "I'm ready, too. Gallows will take me in his boat."

Gallows said, "Eh? What, now?"

The wreck lay a scant mile away as the seagull flies. The canoe and boat, however, took a circuitous route. The waterways swirled around knobs of land arranged like a colossal labyrinth. An hour later, they paddled into a secluded inlet, canoe next to boat. Offshore, the metal prow of the sunken ship angled up from the water's surface, but it was scarcely recognizable.

"It's been dazzle painted!" Brown blurted.

The metal had indeed been painted in blotchy patterns of gray. Projecting railings and riggings had been removed or beaten down. The clear intent was to make the *Sir John Thompson* resemble one of the thousands of rocks that jutted up among the fjords.

Tillamook wrinkled her nose. "Dazzle painted?"

Ace answered. "Dazzle paint is the British phrase. In France, we called it camouflage. Either way, someone wants the *Sir John Thompson* to stay hidden."

Brown said, "Several people."

"Several people with guns," Tillamook added.

Ace's face scrunched. "Indeed. Point taken. Let me call *Sky Arrow One*. It's a beautiful day. They can fly over and be intimidating." Ace raided her pack and began warming up the radio set.

Gallows roused from his petulance to ask, "What people with guns?"

Brown answered, "The people with guns that tried to kill Tillamook and I last time we came here."

Gallows sat up straighter. "Well, now, that's news. But not the sort of news I wanted to hear."

Tillamook fixed Brown with a narrow-eyed stare. "What is this *Sky Arrow One*?"

"Ace Carroway's airship."

"She has an airship. Well, she's got everything."

Brown grew a tender expression as he gazed back. Quietly, he said, "Not everything."

Tillamook's hard expression softened.

Gallows grew more animated. "Wait. Airship?"

"Hush, Gallows."

Ace had her set warmed up and the transceiver stuck in her ear. "*Sky Arrow One*, this is Ace Carroway. Over. ... Come find me. Pinger number three. Is Tombstone aboard? ... Good. Tell him to have his rifle handy. And you, review your protocol about evasive flying. We're at the wreck of the *Sir John Thompson*. Copy? Over. … Over and out."

Ace retracted the antennae and stowed the radio. She dug deeper in her backpack to extract a floppy waterproof suit. She shucked her boots and jammed her legs into the diving outfit. "Let's get set up out there. We'll have air cover soon enough."

Wonder spread over Gallows's blunt face. "Airship. Men with guns. A talking box. A tan, lanky lass named Ace. Pinch me, I'm dreaming."

Brown sent him a quelling glance. "We didn't even mention the underground warehouse full of dead soldiers. Gallows, catch up. There's more going on here than an Irish card sharp chasing a ghost ship."

A giggle escaped Tillamook. "Or chasing Aces."

Chapter 20

Langley stalked out, and the quartet was left alone with Oskar the boat repairman.

"Was it somethin' I said?" Gooper's mustache curved upward in a bristly, and cheeky, expression of delight.

"'Course not, pardner," Tombstone soothed. Then he blinked and amended, "I mean, you shore did mouth off, you ginger gorilla!"

"Love yew too, yew skeletal saurian."

Quack said, "I'm feeling semi-human again. What do we do next?"

Gooper said, "Get Gallows, I say! We're trackin' 'is boat, remember?"

Tombstone said, "Aw, nuts. We shouldda put a pinger in Langley's boat, too. Too late now. Oh, well. Hindsight's always sharper than foresight."

Sam said quietly, "You are right, sahib."

Quack said, "I'm all for tracking Gallows, but we can't just go cruising around in the airship without Ace."

Gooper smacked a fist into an open palm. "Let's get Ace first, then. Off we go."

Oskar stayed seated but raised a hand in farewell. "You really did come in an airship? I hope I get to see it."

"Shore, pardner! It's a wonder to behold. You kin come take a gander right now, iffen you'd like."

"Not now, but soon?"

"Fine. Fine. Y'all take care now, Oskar."

The four men trooped outside the Port Calm general store. They spotted Hulda behind the trading post washing clothes, but they didn't stay to chat. They hurried toward the airship.

Quack said, "Can't wait to change clothes!"

Sam was more sober. "Sahibs, I worry."

"Worry? Don't you have a change of clothes?"

"I have those, Quack." Sam's usual sunny expression appeared thoroughly clouded over. "I worry about Oskar and Langley. Both seemed unreasonable in their reaction to the prospect of visitors. This is unpopulated territory. The average person here is lonely for company. Both men, in different ways, made it clear they wanted no others in the area."

They all trudged uphill for a while.

Tombstone said, "They're hidin' somethin', ya think?"

"I do, sahib. I wish I had more specific insight, but of that fact I am quite sure."

Quack said, "If you think about it, that's true for everybody we've met so far. Brown's a secret Mountie. Gallows is hiding something — or many things. The Hapennys didn't want to admit they were trying to claim this ghost liner as salvage. Now Oskar and Langley."

Sam cleared his throat.

Tombstone looked him up and down. "Son, iffen ya got somethin' on your mind, jes' spit it out."

"Sahib, I do not wish to repeat what may be obvious."

Quack, "Obvious? Sam, just say it."

"It is regarding Oskar. Did you notice his, erm, leg?"

The men exchanged mystified glances. Gooper said, "'E 'ad a blanket over 'is legs, and I wanted one like it. I remember that."

Sam corrected, "Leg, Gooper. He had but one."

Tombstone said, "Huh? One leg?"

Quack said slowly, "As did the man on the ghost liner."

"Was that a living man?" Gooper asked. "'E didn't move."

Sam said, "It is a mystery. It is a possibility. It is a thing to keep in mind."

Gooper said, "Did yew catch Oskar's last name? Or is Oskar 'is last name?"

They trudged along as the question hung in the air.

Quack heaved a sigh. "We're not very good at this detective business, are we?"

Gooper guffawed. "Too true, guv." He slapped Quack on the back, staggering him. "But we make up for our lack of skill wif our copious enthusiasm."

The secret knock to get into the gondola was the Morse code for "ACE.[5]" Gilbert and Vivian were per-

---

[5] A = di-dah, C = dah-di-dah-dit, E = dit.

fectly happy to cast off into the sky to chase Gallows. Vivian especially so, because she missed her hot coffee. If the engines were running, she could brew some.

Before the mooring ropes were loosened, however, the radio crackled. "*Sky Arrow One*, this is Ace Carroway. Over."

Gilbert scooted over the set and toggled the microphone. "*Sky Arrow One*, receiving. Over."

"Come find me. Pinger number three. Is Tombstone aboard?"

"Yes, ma'am."

"Tell him to have his rifle handy. And you, review your protocol about evasive flying. We're at the wreck of the *Sir John Thompson*. Copy? Over."

"Copy. Over."

"Over and out."

Gilbert called back into the lounge, "Change of plan. Finding Ace, not Gallows." The youth caught the eye of the tallest, skinniest one. "Mister Tombstone? Ace said to have your rifle."

"Blimey." Gooper blew air into his cheeks. "I hain't never goin' ter get ter buffet 'is Irish proboscis at this rate."

Gilbert manned the airship controls. Vivian, steaming coffee near her elbow, zeroed in on pinger number three. She rotated the loop antenna to find direction and judged range by the strength of the periodic radio pulse.

The weather continued to improve. The sun shone, and the clouds grew ever fewer. The four associates hung about the lounge, reveling in the feel of dry clothing.

As they gained altitude, Quack tried his hand at improving the nautical map. He peered out various windows, then returned to the chart and penciled in modifications to the shorelines. In some cases, he added new waterways.

In due course, Vivian directed Gilbert to descend. The four associates ran to the control room windows.

Quack said, "I see a boat and a canoe tied to a rock in the water."

Tombstone said, "And a person. A lady-type person."

Gooper huffed air through his mustache. "Yew are a paragon of eloquence, Tombstone."

Tombstone said, "Yep. Oh, I see a man, too, crouching. Working on something. I don't recognize the lady."

Sam said, "Sahibs. That is not a rock. It is a sunken seagoing vessel."

"Whoa," Tombstone said. "It's a big boat."

Vivian said, "We're right on top of the pinger. No sign of Ace?"

Sam gazed a few more moments. "The man is not Mr. Brown. The woman is holding a gun on the man, and the man is pumping air into the diving hoses. I guess Lady Ace and Mr. Brown are below the water's surface."

Quack blinked several times. "Scientific exploration at gunpoint. Now, I've seen everything."

Gilbert pointed more horizontally. "What's that?"

Sam said, "It is a motorized boat, Gilbert."

Tombstone squinted at it. His eyes widened. "Open a window! I gotta get my rifle!"

Tombstone raced back to the lounge. Many of the windows in *Sky Arrow One* could be opened. Sam and Quack unbolted two such and cracked them open.

Gooper peered out at the approaching boat. "Crikey! I see now. Four blokes dressed in green, all with rifles. They're shooting at the girl! Tombstone! Hurry!"

Quack said, "Gilbert! Head toward that motorboat. Give them something to shoot besides the woman on the rock. Erm, ship, I mean."

"Yes, sir," Gilbert said as he pulled a pair of control levers.

Tombstone clattered in with his long-barreled rifle. He promptly stuck it out the window toward the oncoming motorboat and squeezed off a shot. He levered a new shell in and shot again.

"That's done it!" Gooper crowed. "Two shots and they're runnin' like a *Lemmus trimucronatus*[6] from a *Vulpes lagopus*[7]."

The motorboat spun in a half circle of spray and retreated. The men in the boat fired wild bullets at the airship.

Tombstone returned fire, but Quack said, "Back off now, Gilbert. Victory is ours."

---

[6] Lemming.
[7] Arctic fox.

CHAPTER 21

The diving suits were mostly helmets with hoses. The rest of the suit was leaky but hopefully warm. The hoses connected to a hand-operated pump. They prodded Gallows off his boat and onto the wreck.

He said, "I'm to be the draft horse, then? I should have guessed."

"Think of it as repaying one of your past sins," Brown said. Tillamook held the revolver loaded with darts.

Ace said, "It's not hard work, Gallows. It's basically a blacksmith's bellows. The only thing is to keep it going steady."

"Going steady." Gallows wiggled his eyebrows at Ace. "I like the sound of that."

She stared at Gallows with a flummoxed expression. After a moment, she wrenched her gaze to Brown. "The ship lies at a 35-degree pitch but only a ten-degree roll. We'll explore astern and stay on the deck. Ready?"

"I suppose so," Brown said. "Let's see what's below."

They fastened their helmets to their collars with Tillamook's help. Gallows began levering the air pump.

Unceremoniously, the pair headed down the tilted deck and waded into the frigid waters. When their helmets entered the water, air bubbles streamed up behind. One long step later, only the bubbles marked their locations. The hoses coiled at Gallows's feet uncurled and slithered into the water.

Gallows began to sing.

"Well, a landsman's life is all his own.

"He may go or he may stay.

"But when the sea gets in your blood,

"When she calls, you must obey."

Tillamook relaxed among the painted lumps of metal that used to mark the bowsprit of the vessel. "What's your story, Gallows?"

"Me? I'm a perpetual work in progress, that's all. I make things up as I go. So far, I've only been run out of a dozen towns, give or take."

"What a thing to take pride in."

"Ah, no. I'm not so skilled. I have failed to gain a really dastardly reputation." His grin shone white. "But hundreds of towns are left that'll welcome me with open arms, so the future's bright. What about you, lass? You are the happiest sad person I've ever clapped my bright blue eyes on."

"What do you mean?" she replied sourly.

"I'm not quite as dumb as I look, is all. I know 'Tillamook' means 'outcast.' Sure as leprechauns are tricky, you gave yourself that name."

"Better than the name 'Gallows.' You have a death wish, I guess."

"Don't change the subject, lass." Gallows kept pumping as he talked. "You had a home, and now you don't. Why is that? What happened?"

"I don't want to talk about it." Her mouth and voice stayed flat.

"Politics is my guess. You're no hermit by nature,

but pride you've got aplenty."

"Stop guessing. I will tell you this. I can't go home, so I came north. I fish. Or not, sometimes. But I do when I need to eat."

"Fish, eh?" His voice faded to a faraway, dreamy tone. "All right, I have a question. What fish has a great, black fin as tall as me?"

"No fish does, but an orca does." Tillamook frowned at Gallows, who stared raptly out over the water.

Gallows repeated, "An orca. That's a whale, right? But a whale with teeth. Do they eat, uh, for example, divers?"

Tillamook sat up straight. "Trickster! I'm not falling for this! You just want me to look away so you can get the jump on me and run off."

The Irishman pouted. "Lass. Please. I'm a better man than that. At least, I'm trying to be."

Along Tillamook's sight line, past Gallows and the ship, a slippery black back humped out of the water. A tall fin rose and set like a black sun. A moment later, two more whales broke the placid waves and blew clouds of water droplets into the sky.

Tillamook said, "All right, there are orcas."

Gallows wagged his head up and down. "There are a whole lot of them! Is this the orca pub? They're gathering around like we're serving free ale."

Tillamook's eyes darted here and there, seeing evidence of whale everywhere. "Gallows, give those lines a tug. The divers should get out."

"As you command, princess in exile!" Gallows momentarily ceased pumping air and jerked on the air hoses. As he resumed pumping, he emitted a whistle of appreciation. "And here comes an airship, long and silver! What a sight! Whales in the water and a whale in the skies. I'll say it again: I'm a lucky man."

♠ ♠ ♠

Breathing air that smelled of grease and rubber, Ace and Brown descended the sloping ramp of the deck of the wreck. The water level lapped above their helmet visors. In that instant, the ship lay before them, vast compared to the tiny portion that emerged into the air, wrapped in water-shimmer and gloom. The dancing ripples of light illuminated the deck and steel super-structure of the converted troop carrier. Three on a side, gun emplacements dotted the sloping deck, the distant ones fading to the merest shadowy impres-sions.

The advance guard of sea life, sea stars, barnacles, and mussels, clung to the surfaces of the sunken ves-sel. Other than that, the ship appeared seaworthy. The deck was marred by a hole only a few yards further on, the only visible damage.

Whistles and clicks leaked through their helmets, louder than the hiss of air and the bubbling exhala-tions. Wonder spread over the divers' faces. This un-derwater symphony echoed the eerie emanations that had accompanied the ghost liner on its midnight pas-sage. A few steps further on, the cause revealed itself. Sleek, vast shapes moved in the murky waters, graceful in their leisurely explorations. One rolled in a helix, showing its white undersides.

Brown and Ace watched, amazed. Eventually, they turned to each other and touched helmets. Voice loud to herself, faint and tinny to Brown, Ace said, "Orcas!"

Brown nodded, his expression rapt.

Ace said, "I have never heard of them attacking people. Let's go see what's in that hole."

Brown nodded again. They marched downslope to the sole defect in the otherwise flat deck. The ragged hole gaped, about the size of a manhole cover.

The two dragged closer. Their hoses supplied air, which escaped via a one-way valve out the back of their bulbous helmets in a continuous stream of bubbles. Ace tugged more slack as she stepped around the jagged hardwood edge.

They knelt and peered in. Amid a tangle of wooden debris lay a metallic mass, cylindrical and finned like a torpedo. After some moments of inspection, Ace reached in. Extending arms to full length, she grasped the metal cylinder and began pulling. At first, it did not budge. She pulled harder, wiggling from side to side. The heavy object budged, loosened, and eventually yielded.

Ace dragged it up until it peeked out of the hole. Brown helped the rest of way, and they extracted the long object. Overall, it resembled a tank for compressed air, except for the fins at the rear. The front end crumpled in. What appeared to be a nozzle nestled among the fins.

The metal oblong was heavy. They wrestled it sideways and set it against the square base of a capstan so that it would not roll away down the deck.

Brown pointed at a spot on one fin. Battered but recognizable, silvery paint sketched the peaked crown symbol of the Ottoman Empire.

On the fin below that, greenish paint formed the skull and crossbones, with the text "GIFTGAS." Ace's lips moved in the English translation of the German text. "Poison gas."

Ace's air hose tugged sharply. She saw Brown's tighten and release, too. She pivoted upslope to peer back at the surface, but a curious face interposed. A sleek cone of a face, vivid in black and white, and all but filling her field of vision.

The orca turned a bright eye on Ace, then caught her wiggling air hose in its mouth. Ace's eyes flew open. The orca gave a playful squeak like over-stretched rubber and rolled, winding Ace's air hose up around its nose. The action tugged the woman forward, up the inclined deck.

Brown climbed his own hose, hand over hand, toward the massive aquatic mammal. What he intended to do, Ace had little idea, but it seemed like a heroic gesture. For her part, her gloved hands flew to where the air hose connected to her helmet. Frantic, she attempted to wrestle it free.

Just then, the plucks of gunshots rang out, clearly recognizable even underwater.

With an unstoppable pulse of thrust from its flukes, the startled orca bolted, still tightly tethered to Ace.

CHAPTER 22

A bullet pinged off the metal of the bow. Gallows ducked in hope that the mangled remains of the railing would provide some protection. Tillamook threw herself down by Gallows. More shots rang out in the distance as the drone of the airship engines grew louder.

The next moment, the air pump Gallows operated leapt toward the water as if it had suddenly sprouted frog legs. The machine buffeted him at knee and shoulder. Water erupted in a column only twenty feet away, over the wrecked ship. The geyser contained in its midst a black, twisting orca shape. Gallows and the pump slid to the water's edge, only to smack into the stub of a mast. Gallows scrambled to recover the pump as more bullets whizzed overhead.

"A hose broke off!" he cried. "Begorra, who's shooting?" He pulled on the single remaining hose, hand over hand, as droplets from the whale's massive splash rained down.

Tillamook crawled to get a peek at whoever was shooting, but too many things happened all at once. Gallows struggled, knee-deep in brine. The airship zoomed overhead, spitting its own bullets. And then the wave from the crashing whale swamped them both with chill water.

Gallows choked but kept tugging. The wave subsided. The whale disappeared. The humped form of Brown emerged from the water. He flailed at the bolts holding his helmet with one hand, using the other hand to hold the hose.

The flying bullets ceased. Tillamook helped release Brown from his helmet. It popped free. With a metallic clatter, it bounced down the deck to disappear under the waves.

Brown gasped for air. He wheezed, "She's gone! The whale dragged her away!"

The three stared at each other for long moments. As one, they all swiveled to stare at the water. Here and there, a black dorsal fin cut through the waves.

Gallows heaved a long, soulful sigh. "And here I was, gettin' sweet on the lass. Poor thing."

Tillamook sounded surly. "How do the Irish say it? You're a tool, Gallows."

Brown said, "She could be alive. Somehow."

Gallows spotted a whale break the surface in leisurely fashion. A blotch of brown rode its back, ahead of the dorsal fin. It dived again. He rubbed his eyes. "My eyes must be going. But by all the pubs in Dublin, I could swear I saw her riding that whale just now."

"Where?" Brown demanded.

Gallows pointed with a moving finger, tracing the course of the whale.

On cue, the orca broke the surface again. This time, there was no mistake. The splayed limbs of a woman hugged the orca behind its head. As the whale breached into the air, a helmetless, golden head raised up. The head ducked again as the whale exhaled using its blowhole. After the spray, Ace raised to a sitting position. Her hands clutched two strands of the air hose that trailed back from the orca's nose. She threw her head back.

Faint but clear, the three on the boat heard her wild whooping laughter.

The whale dived. Ace flopped flat before disappearing from view.

Gallows said, "That tears it. I'm in love."

Half a minute later, the orca surfaced again. This time, Ace waved. Because it seemed the thing to do, the three on the *Sir John Thompson* waved back. After a quarter minute, the whale dived again, bound on a course away from the inlet, toward a steep-sided island in the middle distance.

Their mutual reverie was broken by an "Ahoy!" from above. Their heads snapped up to see the airship hovering overhead. A blond man leaned out the open gondola door. "Ahoy! Any injuries?"

Brown examined himself, then Tillamook. "Nobody hurt!"

"Very good. We're chasing Ace. Follow us if you like!"

Brown waved and stammered, "Right. Over. Out. Whatever."

Quack flashed a bright smile, waved, and retreated into the gondola. The airship began a slow rise and a ponderous turn.

Gallows said, "I suppose you'll be a-wanting my boat for this chase."

Brown said, "Yes, Gallows. Now, help me out of this thing."

The airship floated away, following the path charted by the whale. They packed up what remained of the diving gear and Ace's pack and attached a tow line to Tillamook's canoe. Gallows fired up the gasoline motor on the *Prince of Wales*.

"I am genuinely impressed," he remarked, "at the sheer amount of trouble you folk've stirred up."

Chapter 23

The airship, and presumably Ace's orca, headed straight for the tall island. Gallows, Brown, and Tillamook buzzed along in last place.

The steep sides of the island approached, rock crags dotted with stubborn trees. The airship sailed over the island effortlessly.

Gallows slowed the motor. "What is this? The whale went straight through the island?"

Tillamook pointed to the left. "There's something there. Try that."

"What, the rock? 'Tis only a rock."

The woman held firm. "The waves do not reflect as they should."

Gallows steered the boat around the stony knob to discover a narrow waterway. The angled channel delved into the island underneath a natural bridge built of piled slabs of gray slate. The watery passage remained deep and wide, with sheer cliff walls on either side.

Gradually, the waterway broadened and the cliffs lowered into more gentle slopes. At the far end of this petite natural harbor lay a one-room cabin and a dock with several boats.

The sight of the largest of them caused Gallows to groan. He clapped hands to grip tufts of his sandy hair. "The ghost liner! In daylight, no less!" The yacht gleamed with white paint and wood tones. It lolled in

147

the sun. Its solidity admitted no hint of ghostly transparency.

A pained expression drew the Irishman's face longer. "Oh, she's so beautiful, but so many eyes are on her. So many eyes."

Tillamook said darkly, "She was never yours, you pirate. Why did you ever think so?"

Gallows said, mournful and slow, "Every rainbow has a pot of gold at the end, they say. I'm the fool that chases after it, but the leprechauns make sure no mortal ever gets it. Grant me this, at least: *this* pot of gold is real and no mere mirage."

Brown said, "She looks more like a luxury yacht than an actual passenger liner. She's not very large, in the light of day."

Tillamook said, "Oskar is there, on deck. With Ace Carroway."

"Oskar?" Brown said.

The Indian shrugged. "Yes, Oskar. He is the local boat repairman."

Gallows gaped. "He's got one leg only!"

Brown raised both of his eyebrows. "He is the ghost captain? The one who stands still as the ghost liner sails?"

"'Twould seem so," Gallows said.

They both glanced at Tillamook. Her face closed tight, but she didn't deny their guess.

A glistening black back and a giant dorsal fin cut across the bow of the little motorboat. A moment later, a blunt head emerged from the waves and chittered at the trio.

Gallows waved at the orca. "How's she cutting?"

The head sank and disappeared.

Tillamook wrinkled her forehead at Gallows. "'How's she cutting?'"

The rangy rogue straightened his back. "'Tis a greeting. We Irish don't *actually* say 'top o' the morning,' you know."

Tillamook stared at Gallows until his roguish grin faded.

A convergence occurred. The airship settled down on the short dock. Familiar men emerged from the gondola to tie the airship down. The little *Prince of Wales* docked there, too, and Brown did the honors of making it fast.

Oskar and Ace awaited both parties on board the ghost liner. Ace wore a dripping flight suit and no boots. Hatless, Oskar showed a balding head to the sun.

"Hello, there, fellas," she said to her associates. "Everybody, this is Oskar. These are Tillamook, Douglas Brown, and Oran O'Gallagher, also known as Gallows. Gooper, don't punch him yet."

Gooper huffed. "Cor! Took the wind right out of me sails, there, Ace. I stand deflated."

Sam peered at Oskar. "Sahib. Are you well?"

Oskar wiped a tear from his cheek and looked at the ground. Only Sam and Tillamook spared glances for Oskar. Everyone else stared at Ace.

Tombstone said, "Well? Spill, Ace! How in tarnation did you rope yerself an orca whale?"

Ace furrowed her brows. "Is that relevant? We need to make plans, and we may not have a lot of time to spare."

Brown said, "I saw the whale take the air hose. When the shots rang out, it leaped out of the water, then swam away like a freight train. And you, Ace Carroway, you were dragged after it by the hose attached to your helmet."

"Spill, Ace," Tombstone repeated.

"All right, all right. The short version, anyway. The orca wanted to play with the hose and wrapped it around its nose. Then it rocketed off. The takeoff was rough, but I held on with both hands. I flopped behind the whale, along its side. Water began filling my helmet. I gulped in what little air I could.

"My first thought was for escape. When the whale slowed, I loosened the helmet. It popped off. I let the rest of the diving suit slide off. It was weighted for diving, so now it's at the bottom of the passage. I kicked for the surface. I *really* needed the air by the time I finally got some."

"Fond of breathing, myself," Gallows said.

"The orca came by again, very slowly, clicking at me and doing barrel rolls."

Oskar said, "It wanted fish."

Ace smiled lopsidedly. "I went with instinct. When the ends of the air hose trailed by, I grabbed them. The orca seemed almost rehearsed. It, not I, parked me on its back." Her eyes lit up. "And then it took off like a trimotor."

Ace focused past infinity and spoke in buttery tones. "It was almost as good as flying."

Gallows, watching Ace, caught his lower lip in his teeth.

Ace inhaled briskly. "I'm sore all over, but it was worth it."

Brown said, "And it swam to … this place. Why?"

Oskar angrily brushed another tear from his eye.

German accents colored his words more than they had in the trading post. "Because the whales are my friends."

Tillamook lifted an eyebrow at Gallows and tried to glare at him, but he was watching Ace.

Brown said, "What do you mean?"

The older man closed his eyes altogether. "They come for food. The fish I give to them. And they come for fun."

Ace snorted. "Fun, for them, perhaps. When the orca threw me into the air, I wasn't amused."

Oskar's face relaxed in fond remembrance. "That is the one called Berlin. He is friendly and playful. The second time, he landed you right here, on deck."

"True. He missed the first time because I flailed like a beginner. But the second time, we made a good team."

Oskar dried his eyes and smiled shyly. "They like to pull the ships. At first, they pulled the smaller ones, but there are more now. More orcas. I net fish in the day, and we play games at night."

Tombstone removed his Stetson to rub his forehead. "Them weird sounds. That was whales? Whales singin' or somethin'?"

Ace gestured thumbs-up to Tombstone. "Just so. They vocalize as they pull the yacht around." She queried of Oskar, "You rigged hoops under the waterline?"

"Yes. The orcas put their noses in and push. They think it is funny. I think it is funny, too. Funny and wonderful."

Sam leaned close. "Sir Oskar, you are desolate. I can see it. Why?"

Oskar's face collapsed, and new tears flowed. "It is the end!" he wailed. His bleary eyes flew to stare at Sam. "My secret is ended."

"Told you so," Tillamook muttered.

Oskar blubbered, "I don't know what will happen, but whatever it is will be bad. Jail, maybe. Maybe they will kill me."

"Who will kill you, Oskar?" Ace asked.

"The Ottomans."

"Ah," Ace said, as if his answer made sense.

Brown said, "But the war has been over for years. The Ottomans lost."

Oskar sniffed contemptuously. "You know little. There are more Ottomans than you think."

Tillamook said, "Remember those guns, Chack?"

Brown clicked his mouth shut with a snap. "Oh, yeah."

Tombstone said, "Uh. I'm lost. What's goin' on?"

Ace grinned. "A summary is in order, Tombstone. But a quick one, because the sun won't stay in the sky forever. Firstly, Oskar's ship. My guess is that it was stolen during the war. Oskar is a deserter."

Oskar patted a capstan affectionately, casting a misty eye over the yacht. "Originally, the ship was Norwegian. The Poles captured it early in the war, and an Ottoman admiral made it his own."

He patted his hip on the empty side. "Bullets took my leg in the first days of the war. After I recovered, my new duty was to be his cook. His yacht, I could not get it out of my head. It drew me like light calls to a moth. One night when I knew the coast wasn't being watched, I sailed it away."

Gallows said, "Smart, I'd say. You stole yourself a

parcel of freedom."

Ace said, "That explains Oskar and his ship. The swamp men represent a different mystery. Let's suppose that the swamp men are the same as the gunmen that guard the wreck of the *Sir John Thompson*. In that case, they have been here for years. They carry German rifles, and they want the wreck to stay secret."

Oskar nodded. "I have heard the whispers in Port Clam. The swamp men speak German when they pick up supplies at night."

Ace gripped the man's shoulder. "Thanks for the confirmation, Oskar. It stands to reason that the swamp men are soldiers left over from the Ottoman Empire. But aboard the wreck of the *Sir John Thompson*, we learned something much more ghastly."

"Wot?" Gooper said.

"We did?" Brown said, bemused.

"Yes," Ace said. "But first, Brown and I stumbled onto an underground storage room. The dead bodies of every sailor and soldier aboard the *Sir John Thompson* lay stacked inside. The clues there included a chemical stench, evidence of primitive autopsies, and a lot of dead beetles and spiders. I guessed poison gas, at the time. But we found proof aboard the *Sir John Thompson*."

Brown scratched at his sideburns. "Oh, that barrel with fins."

Ace's mouth compressed to a dour line. "It's a canister of compressed gas, but fired like an explosive shell from a big gun. One direct hit does not explode and destroy the ship." Her voice came steely and grim. "Instead, it releases a gas so deadly that it kills every living thing on board."

Oskar winced and shuddered. "Things like that. Dark horrors like that are why I defected."

Tombstone's somber face took on a disgusted cast. "Drat Darko Dor anyhow. This hadda be his idea."

Ace ran a hand through her wet hair. "Certainly, Dor, the former Minister of Technology, would have known. It was probably a pet project of his, given his interest in poison gas."

Brown said, "Where did this big gun come from?"

"We cannot know the details," Ace said, "but the crew of the *Sir John Thompson* were killed nearby. My theory is that the suicide governor, Kleine, encouraged the Ottomans to build a base here in the inside passage."

"A base? An Ottoman military base?" Brown's jaw dropped.

"A hidden base, yes," Ace said. "The room with the bodies must be part of it, but there must be more. After the sailors were killed, their bodies were stored in the bunker. The *Sir John Thompson* was still seaworthy at that time. I imagine that the original plan was to capture the ship and crew it with Ottomans instead of Canadians."

"Was it around this time that the Americans declared war?" Brown said. "And Kleine committed suicide."

"Just so. When the tides shifted, so to speak, the Ottomans at the base decided to scuttle the *Sir John Thompson*. They steered it to a lonely spot and poked a hole in the bottom. They had a bit of bad luck in that the prow of the ship remained above water. But this area is unpopulated. It took years for anybody to spot it."

"Namely, Tillamook and I," Brown said.

Tillamook said glumly, "And what will come of it? Only bad things."

Ace said soberly, "I hope not. But now I reach a part near to the hearts of my associates and myself."

"Bert," Quack said, like a thirsty man in the desert yearning for an oasis.

"Bert. We know Bert is near. He left us a note in the death bunker."

Gallows said, "Bert? Here? That means Watts Langley of the ... the secret government office ... base? Begorra!" He clapped hands to his hairline and stared at Ace. "You mean to tell me the Territory of Alaska is paying a thousand dollars a year to maintain a secret Ottoman base? Here, in the exact middle of the back end of nowhere?"

Ace's mirthless smile gave him his answer. Her eyes swiveled over to her associates. "As unlikely as it sounds, fellas, I think Gallows is right. A small, obscure office started by Kleine carries on to this day. It probably supports whatever operations still continue here. Electric service, perhaps. Food and supplies. And apparently a couple of tons of titanium."

"Blimey," Gooper said. "Well, that Langley bloke was awfully miffed when we told 'im we was from an airship."

Ace's mouth was a grim line segment. "That's a good point. 'Miffed' falls short, I'd say. More likely, he's beginning to panic. An airship, yes. And, just now, an airship that chased away a boatful of his gunmen. Marooned Ottoman soldiers, if my guess is right. Langley will have to assume that we know all about the gas cannon because we have examined the wreck."

The flying ace looked from face to face to empha-size her point. "He cannot stand the scrutiny of an in-vestigation. He knows the end of the game is near, whatever game it is that he plays."

"What's the varmint up to, Ace?"

"Poison gas looms large in my mind. What if ..." Ace pursed her lips. "... that gas weapon is their *purpose?*"

Chapter 24

At that moment, Bert labored over sheets of paper on a desk. Langley loomed like a vulture over Bert's shoulder, and he sounded like an angry bee. "Where's the part about no airplanes?"

Bert finished the word he was writing and inked a period after it. Then he tapped three paragraphs up. "In section G, shipping and aeronautics restrictions."

Langley read what Bert had written. "'No vessel upon air or sea shall infringe upon the restricted area whose boundaries are described in section C. This includes law enforcement vessels except to escort trespassing vehicles out of restricted waters or airspace.' Yeah, that sounds all right. And then I see where you list fines and jail time."

"Yes," Bert said dolefully. He massaged writer's cramp from his hands and coughed weakly. The debilitating effects of his time in the chemical-laced morgue lingered. His lungs would recover, in time. The images of the long piles of contorted corpses, however, were seared permanently into his memory.

Now in a crude office in the swamp men's hideout, Bert could breathe. The food and water improved as well. It was also warmer than the charnel house, but his captivity remained as certain as ever. Bert glanced to his right. Sure enough, an alert soldier in a patched Ottoman uniform met his eyes. The fellow aimed a rifle of German manufacture at Bert's chest.

The captive lawyer heaved a sigh and tapped the document with a finger. "I'm done, except for assigning authorship."

"Why do you have to do that?" Langley said.

"All writs and bills have authors and corresponding signatures." Bert spoke patiently. As a prisoner, he had time to spare.

Langley's face stretched in a bitter snarl. "All right. That'll be the governor. Let me worry about that."

Bert doubted the current governor would sign this document, but one never knew. The lawyer had never written a Territorial directive before, much less a fictional one keeping visitors out of this portion of Alaska. He had also never before performed professional services at gunpoint.

"Yah," Bert said. "Am I done here?"

"No," Langley bit off. "Make two copies."

Bert's face drooped in pained resignation.

Footsteps clattered outside. "Oberst! Oberst!"[8]

"What is it now?" Langley growled.

Bert wished Ace were here; her German was fluent. The Bostonian caught about one word in five as a swamp man burst in and narrated in rapid Deutsch.

Langley's face reddened. He blurted, "Two? Lock them up."

Langley switched to German, but Bert caught the word "Hapenny." It reminded him of English coinage.

Before the moss-covered soldier could act, another pair arrived, also bleating, "Oberst!"

"What now?" Langley shouted, putting hands to his

---

[8] German language. Colonel, a military rank.

hair as if about to rip chunks of it off his scalp.

More rapid-fire German commenced, leaving Bert groping. But he caught the word "Luftschiff." The syllables rattled around in his head like thrown dice. Finally, they settled into place, and Bert almost blurted a happy shout. He kept his head down and smiled at the desktop instead. "Luftschiff" meant "airship" or "dirigible." Ottoman soldiers panicked about an airship could mean one thing only: Ace and company were nipping at their heels.

Quack said, "What's the plan, Ace?"

"Pile into *Sky Arrow One*. We'll scout by air until the sun sets."

"What of me?" Oskar said.

Ace said, "Carry on, for now, Oskar. I'm afraid the rumor of the ghost liner is too hot to stop, but you should be all right in the short run. Would you like a radio?"

"A radio?"

"To talk to *Sky Arrow One*."

Oskar considered. He nodded.

"Follow me, pardner," Tombstone said. "I'll unpack a transmitter an' show you how it works."

They all moved from the yacht toward the silent airship tethered to the dock.

Except Gallows. He dragged his feet to let the others pass him on their way to the gangplank. He peeled off the rear of the group to shelter in the doorway of the wheelhouse.

He waited, eyes roving, until the sounds of conversation receded. He smirked and ducked through the wheelhouse to the far side of the yacht, out of sight from the airship. His light eyes darted astern, where the main housing beckoned.

He scuttled crablike to its entrance, then caught his breath as a delighted smile spread across his face. "Exquisite!" he breathed.

A lush dining room lay in panorama before his hungry eyes. Silver candlesticks, platters, and pitchers occupied glass-fronted cabinets around the perimeter. Carved wood panels marched in rows across the ceiling, with brass-fitted tables and chairs beneath.

After a half minute gazing at the opulent display, Gallows shook himself. "The gold will be deeper down. Where are the stairs?"

Seeing no such exits in the dining room, he whirled to face the entrance. He recoiled. "Ay!"

Quack stood in the doorway, arms folded on his chest, lines of disapproval scrunched between his blond eyebrows. "Getting an eyeful?"

The Irishman forced his lips into an upward curve. "Hello, there, lad. No harm in peeking a bit, right?"

"It's trespassing," Quack's rich baritone rolled. "And Ace just told me you knocked Bert out."

Gallows winced. "She did, did she?"

"And if," the blond actor grated out with measured intensity, "the next words out of her mouth hadn't been 'don't injure him yet,' I can assure you you'd be stretched out cold on this hardwood deck by now."

"I believe you, lad."

"Mr. Snana, to you." Quack, known as Boxnard

Warburton Snana on Broadway marquees, unfolded his arms and gestured the Irishman out into the daylight.

"A pleasure, Mr. Snana. They call me Gallows."

"I know. It fits, since I wouldn't object to hanging you by the neck right now."

"Come, come, lad. I'm a reformed character. I have repented. Ask Miss Carroway."

"Gallows, I just caught you wallowing neck-deep in the swamp of greed." Quack wrinkled his nose at Gallows's back as they crossed the gangplank. "What makes you think there's gold on this ship, anyway?"

"Oh, there is," Gallows crooned. "Even if this Oskar lad says there isn't. Even if he's never seen it. Maybe the ballast is made of gold bars."

"That's …" Quack glanced at Gallows as they entered the airship's shadow. "… crazy, Gallows."

"Nay, lad. Not when you need a dream to cling to. Somewhere, there's a pot of gold for me. There must be."

They walked yards further before Quack replied. "Shift your dream, Gallows. The mania of owning things only eats at one's spirit. What seems so seductive is poison in the end."

Gallows rounded on Quack and snarled, inches from his face, "Shut up. It's easy for you to say, with your tweed coat and your fancy airship. You never had *nothing* like I've had all my life, Mister Snana."

"You think so?" Quack murmured, holding his ground.

Gallows wavered. "Aye. And your good looks. And your *Ace*." The Irishman grimaced. "Is she your girl?"

Quack's eyebrows rose. "Of course not. She's—"

"Good," Gallows barked. He pivoted and marched toward the *Sky Arrow One* gondola. He stomped up the ladder, leaving Quack behind.

The actor paused where he was and shook his head ponderously. "How to explain?" he muttered under his breath. "It's not *like* that."

He raked a glance over the silvery aircraft and the beckoning skies beyond. "It's better."

The fjords sparkled from the air. Shadows lengthened as the afternoon wore on. The waters painted themselves a deep sapphire blue between fingers of pine green forest.

"Beautiful," Brown said.

Tillamook said, "Thank you, Chack." The pair exchanged glances, eyes dancing. "But I can see Oskar's dock, plain as the brown man's fuzzy side fur. How could something so obvious be hidden?"

"Ground squirrels see the world differently than hawks," Ace said. "Ten degrees port, Vivian."

"Yes, ma'am."

Ace tapped Brown's shoulder. "Brown, look starboard. See the square of lighter green on the flank of the peninsula?"

"Yes."

"Underneath is where the bunker lies. It's possible to spot with sufficient foreknowledge."

Brown grunted. "I see! So, we're looking for similar patches?"

"Perhaps. Anything artificial."

Tillamook pointed out the window. "Well, I see something over that way."

"Good job. That's Port Clam."

"Ah."

Sam interjected, "I see a large ship."

Ace said, "Thirty-five degrees port, Vivian."

"Yes, ma'am."

Gallows said, "You're all eagles, and I'm a vulture. I can't see it."

Sam said, "It is gray and partially shadowed. It is moored next to a very tall cliff. It has one very large gun facing forward, three machine gun emplacements in the stern, and two machine gun emplacements amidships."

Ace said, "Confirmed. Good eye, Sam."

Tillamook said, "It's only maybe three miles from Port Clam, though you have to cross two ridges to get there."

Ace extended a brass spyglass reminiscent of mariners of yore and peered through it. "Hold position, Vivian."

"Yes, ma'am."

"I think I see the hideout. It's built into the cliff. Or perhaps I should say that they gave the cliff a façade. A façade disguised as a cliff."

Sam added, "Overlooking the ship."

Quack asked, "Does the ship have poison gas?"

Ace said, "We can only assume that it does. We must also assume that the cliff hideout has a supply. All right, Vivian, drop us into shadow."

"Yes, ma'am."

Ace folded her spyglass. "We have enough information for at least a Gooper-style plan."

Tillamook and Brown exchanged a mystified glance.

Gooper preened his mustache. "Music to me ears. We get ter blow something up, then?"

"No, not *that* Gooperlike. Just flamboyant. I think we should scale the cliff from behind and drop down the face on ropes. We'll enter the hideout via the top-level windows."

Quack said, "And find Bert?"

"And find Bert."

"Hot diggety!" Tombstone said.

Ace's eyes sought out Brown, Tillamook, and Gallows. "My associates and I are about to poke a hornet's nest. You three should stay out of it, I think."

Gallows puffed his chest out and raised a finger into the air. "Now, lass, I've been a second-story man for a month of Mondays, and—"

His words cut off due to Gooper. With a flex of his mighty chest and bunching of shoulder muscles, the rugby center drove a pile driver of a fist into Gallows's face. The Irishman catapulted backward into the weather instrument bank. He bounced, then flopped to the metal floor, face-first.

Gooper blew cooling air through his mustache and across his knuckles. He winked. "There. Job done. Timing seemed about right."

Sam said, "Impeccable, sahib."

Quack smiled faintly. "Bravo."

Tombstone nudged the collapsed rogue ungently with the toe of his cowboy boot. "Good fer you, Gooper. Every time he calls you 'lass,' Ace, I jes' see red. You ain't no li'l slip of a girl, nohow, calendar age notwithstanding."

Ace said, "I appreciate that, Tombstone. Respect is what makes our team work. Speaking of team, though …" She clapped a hand on the blond actor's shoulder. "Quack? Are you all right?"

Quack's attempted sunny expression faltered. "Well enough. If we don't find Bert soon, though, I think I'll either explode or collapse."

Tombstone nodded. "I hear ya, pardner."

Brown cleared his throat. "I thought about staging a protest, but I changed my mind. I can sit this one out."

Tillamook said, "Yes, you can."

CHAPTER 25

Sky Arrow One skimmed the wavetops in the twilight. On a roundabout course, it approached the cliff hideout from the rear.

Quack, Gilbert, and Ace had gradually amended the nautical map. They charted waterways and marked landmarks such as "death bunker" and "ghost liner dock." The newest label was "poison ship dock," and the associates dressed for trouble.

Brown caught a glimpse of Tombstone pulling a dark sweater over what resembled a gold metal shirt. "What was that gold?" the Mountie asked.

"Chain mail undershirt. Ace's invention. She says she ain't done with the design, but this version stops bullets, mostly. It shreds the bullets into li'l pieces and some o' them pieces still get through. So it hurts like the dickens — but you don't die."

"Not dying sounds like a good thing. Very clever."

Tombstone dislodged his Stetson to rub his temple ruefully. "History has shown we get shot at a lot. Now, a hole in the head might benefit Gooper over there, but the rest of us, we have thinkin' to do."

"I 'eard that, yew desiccated beanpole!"

"Gnarly ginger root."

"Overgrown twig."

"Musclebound throwback."

The pair's traded barbs represented only background noise for Quack and Sam. They pocketed compact sidearms loaded with anesthetic bullets. Another of Ace's inventions, the hollow bullets did not penetrate deeply into flesh but released a sleep-inducing drug. Ace's version produced unconsciousness faster than Brown's curare-laced version.

Ace herself donned a black flight suit with a wide belt. As Vivian set the gondola down on a tiny sandbar, Ace offered Gallows an ice pack. "Gallows, here's something to make you feel a little better."

"Ah, fair colleen. The comfort you give." He gingerly mashed the cool bag against his purpling cheek.

Ace smiled lopsidedly. "Score's all tied, now, with the fellas. They won't hold a grudge."

"And you?"

The pilot clasped her hands behind her back and bounced on the balls of her feet. Her eyes roved around the cabin. "Your information on Watts Langley crystallized the whole case."

"Not that." The Irishman seemed subdued, steady, and sincere. "Do I have a ghost of chance at courtin' ye?"

Ace met his eyes. "I can't let all that mushy stuff cloud my head. See you soon, Gallows."

The party of five crept to the cliff's edge. The sun had long set, but the moon had not risen. Only starlight illuminated the slender bulk of the warship below. Faint boot stomps, metallic clanks, and brisk calls could be heard from the ship.

Sam whispered, "There is a foot path here along the clifftop. There may be sentinels."

Ace said, "Let's string the ropes. Quack, guard the knots up here."

"Blast," the actor kvetched. "Why me?"

"Logic. Your cool nerves, your killer instinct. The fact that you're not a loose cannon like Gooper."

Gooper emitted a sound like a deflating bullfrog.

Quack raised his palms in resignation. "I hate to miss the fun. But, all right. I'll guard the back door."

In silence, they secured the ropes to trees. Clips connected their belts to the ropes. All but Quack began creeping backward down the cliff, feeding slack rope through the metal clips.

Sam suffered and sweated, but his death grip on his rope never wavered, and he descended to the first row of windows without incident. The recessed windows resembled the arrow slits in the castle walls of yore. But these windows were wider, with glass panes. By the time Sam reached them, Ace had already engraved a glass cutter circle on a pane. She pinched her double mint gum out of her mouth and stuck it on the pane, then tapped. The pane popped inward, arrested by the sticky gum. Ace grabbed it more securely, then slithered inside.

The window by Sam opened. Ace stuck her head out. "All clear in here. Come on in."

"Easier said than done, Lady Ace."

Ace reached out, hooked him by his belt, and brought him into the recess. "Get your legs in. Good. Now let go of the rope."

Sam frowned at his hands. They stayed clutched, straining and beginning to tremble.

Ace said, "You can do it. You always find a way, Sam. I've got you. I won't let you down."

"Oh. Oh, my. Here I go."

Sam unclenched. The rope relaxed as he took his own weight on his feet. Ace hooked his arm and steadied him. She lightly punched his shoulder. "Wheels down safe, my friend."

"Yes, memsahib. And where do we find ourselves?"

Black masses indicated that Tombstone and Gooper were already present.

"These are sleeping quarters." Ace unclipped Sam from his rope. "More interesting rooms must lie below. Let's find the stairs."

Tombstone said, "Everything's dark. Mebbe they don't have 'lectricity here."

Sam rubbed feeling back into his hands. "It is very quiet."

The party diffused into the barracks, feeling their way for the most part. The starlight filtering through the widely spaced windows did nothing to illuminate the interior.

A bump sounded. "Crikey! Me knee!" Gooper blurted.

"Shh!" Tombstone hissed.

Everyone froze, listening. But there seemed no sign of life. They resumed searching.

Quack nibbled on his own lower lip and gazed out and down on the warship. Occasionally, little pools of light would wander around below, men carrying electric torches on the ship's deck and nearby dock. He heard only the buzzing of a few insects and the calls of night birds.

It felt like hours, but it must have been only minutes since the party disappeared over the cliff. Quack rubbed sweaty palms on his thighs. A flicker in his peripheral vision captured his attention. Sparks rose from the smokestacks of the ship, faint but distinct in the starry night.

"They've fired up the boilers! They're leaving." Quack's brow furrowed as he stared. "How long does it take to get a good head of steam? Is everyone on board? Is that why there are no sentinels?"

A new blob of light below attracted his attention. Electric torches shone on three figures, shuffling up the gangplank onto the ship. Rifle silhouettes pointed at the hapless people, two men and a woman. Their hands were tied behind their backs. The slimmer man had a particularly erect carriage and a crisp stride.

"Bert," Quack breathed. "Found you. And I guess the Hapennys sailed into the wrong cove. Ace, where are *you*? Do you see?"

Quack's fists clenched as he inwardly debated.

Half a minute later, Quack went from frozen to frantic. He yanked a rope up and tied another to it, making it double length. Sparing but one glance to chart his course, he backed out over thin air. Risking rope-burned palms, he descended the cliff face like a two-legged spider on a thread.

Chapter 26

Ace and company worked the Ottoman hideout from top to bottom, largely by sense of touch. Not a single soul did they meet in the whole base. The hidden installation contained bunkrooms, common rooms, kitchen, bathrooms, and even a library. The lowest level contained a room with jail cells, but the cells were empty.

Ace fretted, "This is taking too long. The moon is rising by now, and that vibration in the floorboards quit. Where is the front door?"

"I found a door," Tombstone drawled.

"I found an electric torch," Sam said.

They followed Tombstone's voice to a front-facing wall. The cowboy turned the knob and cracked the door open.

Silence.

Darkness.

Stillness.

He opened the door wide. They stepped out onto a wooden dock. Trees towered, blocking the horizon in all directions except the cliff's. The moon outlined in silver the cliff, the dock, and the distant trees. The water off the edge of the dock glimmered.

The warship was gone. No sign of movement could be discerned. A faint, ghostly trail of smoke lingered in the placid night air over the open end of the U-shaped island.

"Oh, ugh," Ace said. "How could something so foolhardy and rash end up so perfectly safe and anti-climactic?"

"They all left? Every one?" Gooper said.

Ace said, "I guessed we had them panicked. I didn't guess *how* panicked. They've gone on the run, on a fully armed and recognizably Ottoman ship."

Tombstone rubbed his long, stubbly chin. "An' Bert?"

"He might be on that ship."

"And if not?"

"If not, I don't want to think about it."

Sam clicked the switch on his electric torch and played its beam around the area. It was nearly expired, but it supplemented the growing moonlight.

Ace said, "Sam, point that torch out there."

Sam followed Ace's pointing finger. Past the space where the warship had hulked, the dim rays showed a row of boats. One of them was Watts Langley's small motorboat. The next—

Gooper blurted, "Hoy! That's the boat of the man and wife, the Hapennys."

Ace said, "Oh, no. Really?"

Tombstone said, "Uh-oh."

Ace paced back and forth like a caged cat. "There is much we don't know. I want to chase the warship while the trail is warm. But they have mounted machine guns. *Sky Arrow One* would be shot down before it got close."

Ace turned toward the cliff face and called, "Quack!"

Sam said, "Memsahib. I think Quack is not there."

"What? Why not?"

Sam played his light on the side of the cliffside hideout. A slender braid lay vertically against the wall, ending in a loose coil on the ground. "I see a rope dangling here. It could only be Quack's."

Tombstone said, "He came down here? Why?"

Sam said, "Sahib, my mind grows more and more sure: Quack has left us to ride the Ottoman ship."

"Tarnation!" Tombstone spat.

Ace said, "Then we'll chase the ship. Somehow, we've got to get aboard without getting shot to Swiss cheese."

From her back, she unslung her portable radio and extended its antenna. She waited a few more moments as the vacuum tubes warmed up.

Sam stroked his neat little curled mustache. "It is dark. And the Hapenny boat is fast."

Everyone paused to regard the diminutive archaeologist.

Quack darted down the dock, light-stepping like a dancer. Dark shapes called tense phrases in German aboard the warship. The blond actor pulled his dark hat down tighter over his head and scurried on. Under cover of darkness, his vague shape should be indistinguishable from any other.

"Don't collide with anyone, now," he muttered. At last, the gangplank materialized out of the gloom. Quack discovered that merely wishing for weightlessness, no matter how earnestly, did nothing to affect his mass. His footfalls rang the metal ramp like a dull bell.

Grimacing at the cacophony, he hurtled through the gap in the iron railing onto the deck of the warship. From forward, a nasal baritone cut through the air.

"Baumann?"

Instinct turned Quack away from the voice. As he strode aft, he lifted a shoulder and pressed his mouth to it. Thus muffled, he grunted a deep, "Nein!"

Heart thudding in his chest, he controlled his pace to a walk. Two steps. Three. Four.

No pursuit. A row of landing boats loomed to Quack's right, stacked on their sides. He darted to them and squirmed his way between a pair. He slithered to a tense crouch between the hull of one and the benches of the next, vulnerable but hidden. Steel clad most of the ship, but the boats were wooden. Judging by the smell, they were also partially rotten.

Quack panted, trying desperately to do so quietly. But no one passed the gap between boats that he could see.

In the minutes he waited to regain his wind, the gangplank raised and the warship began to vibrate. He squeezed forward until he could peek out.

No human shadow moved, but the cliff face drifted by, dead slow. The ship was underway. Quack frowned and counted the boats. His eyes swiveled to gun turrets left and right, but they lacked gunners. He mused under the dull sounds of boilers and turbines coming from below. "The ship's built for a hundred crewmen, if not two hundred. But there can't be nearly that many aboard."

His eyes darted forward, to the main superstructure

of the ship. "So maybe Bert and those other people aren't guarded. Where would the brig be? Down deep, I'd guess."

On tiptoe, he skulked forward. Dim, unsteady electric lights lit a doorway from within. Quack crept past the thick steel door, swung wide open. The passage within split three ways, but the forward path dove down ladderlike stairs.

The lump of his pistol rode in his front pocket. But one shot would bring the whole ship of swamp men down around his ears. He left it in his pocket, to lessen the temptation of using it.

He patted the radio pinger in his back pocket. Sooner or later, Ace and crew would follow its signal, and it would lead them to the warship *and Bert.* Buoyed by the thought, he forged ahead and down, through patches of gloom and islands of electric light. Streaks of rust and peeling paint coated the metal walls of the narrow passage.

The stairs ended in a left-right choice, and Quack chose the right-hand companionway. The turbines and screws roared louder down here, and Quack's ears strained to detect enemy footfalls.

An open door loomed ahead on his left, unlit and cavernous. He stuck his head inside. Dim rows of metal barrels like oil drums sat in stacks, held in place by steel racks.

"Huh. Cargo." Quack's hopeful face fell. He forged ahead like an ancestral hunter, glad that he had oiled the leather of his boots. No leathery squeak did they emit as he padded along.

He approached a crossroads.

But he froze in place. Footfalls approached, clomp-

clomping on the steel floor. Shadows flickered up ahead.

Quack quick-stepped forward and hugged the left wall. The clomping grew in intensity. He balled his fists and tensed tighter.

A bulky man rounded the corner, taller and far rounder than the actor. His military-cut hair, blunt face, and meaty hands were exposed to the air. Blotchy moss covered the rest of him so that he resembled a walking swamp.

Quack punched the fellow in the gut.

The force of the blow dissipated in the moss coating and layer of flab. The man grunted and squinted at Quack in disbelief.

The actor swung a left uppercut to the jaw. It connected, and the swamp man's eyes all but rattled in their sockets. Unlike a trained boxer, the giant kept his hands low. He slapped one to his belt and palmed a knife.

"Oh, no," Quack muttered as he swung a right hook.

His massive adversary punched him in the chest, driving the point of the blade straight in. The force of the thrust pushed Quack back against the steel bulkhead, but the point of the knife slipped. With a metallic rasp, it sliced through the actor's dark sweater and struck sparks from the metal mesh beneath.

On the rebound, Quack tried again, punching desperately at the taller man's jaw, first a right, then a left.

The portly moss man's eyes glazed. He toppled. His knife skittered free.

Quack panted for a few moments, then grabbed a fistful of moss-shirt. In spurts, he dragged the heavy fellow aft. "Where to stash him?" Quack muttered.

The actor paused to collect the fellow's knife and adjust his own hat. "Where he can't be found. Where's that, then? Overboard, I guess."

GUY WORTHEY

CHAPTER 27

The four stumbled in the gloom to board the Hapennys' craft, the *Violet*. Ace spoke over her transmitter as they walked. Vivian reported that Quack's pulse transmitter was on and that Oskar had been in touch via radio.

"Good. Confirm that the warship and the pinger location are one and the same. Launch *Sky Arrow One*. Tail the ship but stay at least five hundred yards up. They are liable to shoot at you otherwise. Over."

"Copy, Ace. We'll stay high."

"You follow them, and we'll follow you in the *Violet*. If we neutralize the ship, we'll let you know."

"Copy."

"Over and out."

Tombstone said, "Sam, gimme that light. We ain't goin' nowhere iffen there ain't any gas in the tank."

But the *Violet* had fuel, and the motor was willing.

Tombstone flicked the electric torch around the wheelhouse. "No bodies. No blood."

"That is good news, sahib."

They cast off. Ace assumed control of the wheelhouse. The chase was on.

Gooper mimed a boxer throwing punches. "'Ere we go, then. David chasin' Goliath."

Tombstone drawled, "A june bug tacklin' a Texas longhorn."

Sam said, "An ant attacking, er, something larger

181

and more fearsome than an ant."

Ace said, "All right, fellas. I love you all, but shush. Find all the loose ropes you can, and improvise some grappling hooks."

"Immediately, memsahib!"

"Tombstone, do you have your rifle?"

"Yes, ma'am."

"Gooper, did I see grenades on your belt?"

"Yew know it."

"Sam?"

"I did not know those were grenades, memsahib. I took no notice, thinking merely that Gooper displayed his own unique fashion style."

"No, Sam, not that. Did you bring your pocket hammerless?"

"Ah, the semiautomatic pistol. Yes, I have it. However, my marksmanship skills are those of a beginner, as I think you know."

Tombstone said, "Sam, bless your heart, you kin barely hit a haystack at ten paces."

Ace said, "If shot at, I'd like us to return fire, that's all. I found a shotgun up here. I'll take that."

♠ ♠ ♠

Quack managed to get the flabby swamp man up the stairs and out on deck. The actor snatched an O-shaped life preserver from the rail and tied it around the unconscious fellow. Unceremoniously, Quack heaved him over the railing. Mostly, the engine noise and rush of wind covered the splash sound.

He rubbed his own aching arms. "That was a lot of work. But, one down. How many to go? Twenty?"

But an annoyed voice called, "Baumann? Schmidt?"

The sound threw a jolt of electricity up Quack's spine. Before conscious thought could kick in, his legs ran for the door down belowdecks.

The owner of the voice followed. As Quack clattered down the stairs, it repeated, "Schmidt? Baumann?"

As Quack hit the flat at the bottom, the voice barked, "Halt!"

The trim actor had no such intention. He slowed abruptly at the open door to the cargo hold and bolted into the darkness. A dozen paces in, the edge of a rack clipped him across the eyebrow with a jab of hot pain.

Quack stifled a cry and felt for a gap between racks of barrels. His hasty plan was to lie in wait. His pursuer may pass on by or come inside. If the latter, the blond actor would prepare to pounce.

A helmeted shape paused in the doorframe. Moss hung from his steel cap, but a shabby, plain Ottoman uniform clad the rest of him. The flabby one had been armed only with a knife, but this skinnier man cradled a rifle.

Blood dripped into Quack's eye, forcing him to blink. When he looked again, the soldier's silhouette had vanished.

Quack's forehead furrowed in the darkness. Had the soldier moved on? Or did he lurk in the gloom the same as his quarry?

The click of an electric relay clarified the matter. Distant light bulbs flared. Their dim light was enough for Quack to see the soldier raise his rifle and aim it squarely at Quack's chest.

With the light on, Quack could spot a few places to duck but nowhere to run. He was cornered.

But the soldier backed out the door, still holding his rifle aimed at Quack's heart.

The soldier abruptly shouldered his rifle and seized the door to swing it shut.

Quack sprinted for the exit, but he was far too late. With a deep clang like a kettle drum, the steel door slammed shut.

"Ugh," Quack said as he pressed on the unyielding door and fruitlessly twisted the locked latch.

Shoulders drooping, he listlessly explored. The ceiling was high, but the racks of barrels ascended almost to the top. Lanes of various widths opened sideways, and, except near the door, the floor plan degenerated into a maze. The cargo was monotonous: barrel after barrel on top of barrel after barrel.

A high keening wailed over the vibration of the engines. Quack's shoulders hunched, and he darted his gaze around in wild alarm. The ghostly sound resembled the hollow sound of a woman crying, echoing in the vast metal box.

His teeth grated together. "I'm turning heyoka[9]."

But a few twists of the maze later, the sobbing replayed. This time, his ears picked out a direction, and he crept around a rack of barrels, the back of his neck tight with tension.

A collection of brown-gray lumps on the floor broke the geometric regularity of the stacks of steel

---

[9] He means that he is turning contrary to reality, like the Heyoka ceremonial figure.

cylinders. One of the lumps moved, and Quack sucked air between tight teeth. The lump resolved into the head of a woman with fear-widened eyes.

Bette saw him and gasped. Metal chains jingled.

A lump to her right rolled and raised. It was a man, face darkened by several days' growth of whiskers and hollowed-out eye sockets. Boston accents brayed, "Quack? Is that you? Wicked glad to see you, chum." And then Bert fell victim to a fit of coughing.

The watercraft chase unfolded in slow motion. Tentative wisps of fog condensed, and the rising moon transformed the forested islands into fantasy sky-scapes. Half-seen ships, ghost vessels all, glided along the gossamer web of waterways. But the most spectral vehicle of them all sailed the atmosphere above in seeming defiance of gravity and common sense.

After his first-time nerves calmed, Oskar liked the radio. He called *Sky Arrow One* frequently. "Your voice is young," he told Gilbert. "I have a son. If he survived the war, he would be seven years old."

Gilbert sat at the radio station, and Vivian controlled the helm. They exchanged a glance, the inscrutable communication of twins.

"Yes, sir," Gilbert replied into the microphone.

After a brief, sheepish silence, Oskar radioed, "How is it with Ace Carroway and the Ottoman base?"

Gilbert relaxed. "The Ottomans are running away,

we think. They are on a large warship. Mr. Quack and maybe Mr. Bert are on board. We have them in view, but we are staying high in case they shoot at us. I'm not sure we can maintain visual contact very long. There is increasing fog. Over."

"Is Ace Carroway on board your airship?"

"No, sir. She and three detectives chase the warship in a small boat."

"What? What are they going to do?"

"I don't know, sir. Rescue Mr. Quack, somehow."

"It won't work. They'll be shot to pieces."

Gilbert and Vivian exchanged glances again. Gallows hovered at the bulkhead between control cabin and lounge.

Oskar spoke again. His voice sounded oddly strained. "Which direction are they heading?"

"South, sir. Ace said they may possibly be trying to reach Seattle."

"That sounds bad. Is the ship full of poison gas?"

"I don't know, sir."

"Are they … are they going to pass my island?"

Gilbert checked the ever-improving navigation chart. "Yes, sir. They will have to if they continue going south. Their ship is only making about twelve knots, though, so it will be twenty minutes or twenty-five."

Oskar's strained vocal tones continued. "Thank you, *Sky Arrow One*. I'll stop talking now. Bye bye."

"Over and out, sir."

There was quiet for half a minute.

Gallows had been listening as he loitered behind the navigator's cubby. "That," he observed, "was the voice of a desperate man. Take it from a lad who's been there."

Vivian and Gilbert glanced back at Gallows, then at each other.

Gilbert said, "Yes, sir."

"I could hear him sweating when he asked about the gas." Gallows grinned, then said, "Ow!" He clapped a hand to his aching face and wobbled back to the lounge.

Another half minute passed. Vivian said, "Fog's thickening. I lost sight of the ship for a few seconds there."

Gilbert said, "Pulse transmitter is steady and strong. We won't lose them."

Vivian said, "Yes, but Ace might lose sight of us."

Up in the tall, open wheelhouse of the *Violet*, Ace clenched her teeth. "I lost sight of the *Sky Arrow*! The fog's getting thicker."

Gooper said, "Crikey! Well, here's 'opin' we catch good luck. We're closing in, aren't we?"

Ace mentally estimated the angle from horizon to airship. "Yes. A furlong or two. You made skyhooks?"

Tombstone said, "Yep. Two. You can tell them Hapennys were miners. They had a couple o' pickaxes down in the bilge. We tied 'em to ropes."

Gooper said, "Nice, heavy pickaxes."

"I like it. What I don't like is being second on deck, but I guess somebody has to drive the boat."

A sudden clammy chill announced the arrival of a

fogbank. They sped on, blind, unable to see beyond the *Violet*'s bowsprit.

"Cor," Gooper remarked.

Seconds ticked by, then a whole minute. Ace held the helm fixed.

Sam said, "Under the noise of our own engine, I think I hear the churning and splashing of a large screw."

Ace said, "Collision is possible. Be ready."

Soon, everyone could hear the low throb and gush of the warship's engines.

"I am on pins and needles, my friends," Sam squeaked.

"I hear their screw. I'll navigate by sense of sound." Ace clocked the wheel a few points starboard. "Get ready with the grappling hooks."

The fog cleared. The moon revealed a clear scene, dominated by the hulk of the warship. The *Violet* rode in the wake of the larger ship, closing fast, but too far starboard. Behind lay the fogbank they had just left. Ahead lay a new curtain of mist. To the sides, forested ridges adorned the horizon.

Abruptly, the slow pace of unfolding sped up. Ace spun the wheel to port. The *Violet* veered toward the warship. Ace barked, "It's got railings. And it's running very low in the water. Ready to board?"

"Ready, Ace!" Gooper said, hefting a pickaxe and its dangling rope. Tombstone brandished an identical one.

Shreds of fog flitted by. Visibility declined.

All eyes but Sam's were fixed on the warship. It did ride low in the water, as if heavily loaded. Its railings should catch the improvised grappling hooks with ease. But movement caught Sam's eye. Ahead of the warship, a streamlined shape mingled with the mists. Its elegant profile moved silently forward.

"The ghost liner!" Sam cried.

"What? Where?" Ace said.

"Ahead, memsahib! Dead ahead!"

A gray-black wall of metal rose up ahead and to their left as mists raced by. Ace hesitated only a moment. She cried, "Full stop!" and yanked the throttle to zero.

For one and only one heartbeat, the *Violet* coasted forward. The fog enclosed them impenetrably. Each stood isolated on a private circle of deck that extended a mere dozen feet before being swallowed by the thick vapors. The wet, cold air wrapped around them like the deathly embrace of a vengeful spirit.

The next heartbeat brought a subsonic boom that gripped the air in its teeth like a colossal dog and shook it back and forth with stupendous power. The bone-shaking crash reverberated in water and ear. Only the end of the world could be louder.

In the next instant, the gray wall of the side of the warship leaped at them from out of the mist. Inexorably, it bore down on the *Violet*. Though the booming of the first unseen catastrophe continued, there was a second crash as the *Violet* impacted the warship. Water sprayed and hardwood splinters flew.

Sam, Tombstone, and Gooper lost their footing and tumbled forward. Dauntless, they scrambled to their feet. The railing of the warship loomed above them. Tombstone and Gooper recovered their pickaxe skyhooks. Swinging as one, they lofted the pickaxes high. The warship stern rode high but ponderously descended. The pickaxes hit the warship deck and bounced. Via good luck or skill, the grappling hooks slid between the deck and rail and plopped back inside the *Violet*. The small ship sloshed in the wave caused by the dropping stern, but Gooper and Tombstone each managed to tie off their ropes.

"Did it! Did it!" Gooper crowed.

"Hot diggety. Let's git on up there!"

Sam said, "Very skillful of you, gentlemen. Do you agree, Ace?"

Gooper and Tombstone scrambled up their rope ladders to the warship deck, grunting as they pulled up hand over hand.

"Ace?"

Chapter 28

The infantryman pelted into the engine room and almost collided with the engineer. "Lock the door," the infantryman blurted in German. "Quickly!"

"What? Put that gun down." The engineer rubbed his chin.

"There's a man in the cargo hold, dumb-dumb. Lock the door!"

The heavyset engineer lumbered toward a windowless steel door at the aft end of the engine room. "A man? What man?"

"How am I supposed to know? A spy. I chased him in there. Lock it before he gets out."

"Fine, fine." The engineer grasped the central of three steel wheels that served as latches for the heavy door. "Not closed very well," he remarked.

The infantryman pointed his gun at the door as if it had become a target. "Not? Why not? Did anybody come out of there?"

The engineer spun the smaller wheels, first the top, then the bottom. Unseen deadbolts slid into steel sockets. "No. I'm sure I would have seen."

The infantryman eyed the towering boilers, the spaghetti of pipes and ducts, and the roaring fuel oil burners. "Are you absolutely sure?"

The boom of a warship-sized bass drum assaulted their ears. The engine room rocketed backward and threw the men forward. Electric speakers squawked, only a little louder than the ringing of their ears, "Full stop! Full stop!"

Unseen behind a row of oversized valves, a slender blond man braced himself against the sudden deceleration. He muttered in English, "Thunder to rival that of the Wakinyan. Did Ace conjure that up, somehow? Or did we run headlong into an island?"

The titanic rumbles decayed. The warship stayed on an even keel, and its engines quieted. Ace had vanished from atop the wheelhouse and did not respond to Sam's plaintive call.

"Cain't wait," Tombstone said mournfully as he threw a long leg over the warship's railing.

"But—" Sam said, his worried head questing.

The fog relented enough to dimly see about half the deck of the warship. After tying the *Violet* fast, Gooper and Tombstone fumbled and flipped over the warship's rail. Painfully, they tumbled to the deck. Tall smokestacks and their square housings filled the middle of the ship. Machine-gun turrets dotted the deck edges, but no gunners manned them.

But that was the end of the good news.

"*Warnung!*" rapped out a voice amidships. Bullets whizzed. Gooper and Tombstone scrambled for cover at the rear of the smokestack housing.

Tombstone unlimbered his long-barreled rifle from his back. "Awright, we conquered a quarter of the ship already. Two thirds to go."

"Oi like your math," Gooper retorted. He reached to his belt and plucked a miniature grenade from it. His fingers were almost too blunt to remove the pin, but he managed it. He ducked his head around the housing.

Two men dressed in Ottoman infantry uniforms swiveled their guns at him. He threw his grenade wildly and yanked his red head back to safety.

A sharp pop sound announced the grenade explosion, a microscopic tick compared with the gigantic boom from a few minutes ago. Nevertheless, when Gooper snuck a peek, he saw a lone soldier in full retreat.

He crowed, "Har! I knocked one overboard!"

From the other corner, Tombstone called, "Keep it up! Tell you what, this sharpshootin' rifle ain't 'xactly the best tool fer a firefight, but I guess I'm makin' 'em keep their heads down. Hey, where's Sam an' Ace?"

♠ ♠ ♠

Up in the wheelhouse, Ace discovered too late that she was insufficiently braced. When the *Violet* crashed against the iron wall of the warship, the high wheelhouse amplified its snap. Like a lacrosse ball released from its stick, Ace hurtled into space.

She plummeted out of control on an arc, well past the deck of the *Violet*. Messily, she splashed into the space between the *Violet* and the warship.

The wall of frigid water shocked her skin to pinpricks. Her diaphragm clenched like an iron vise. She forced numbed hands to unlace her boots as her body tumbled beneath the waves. Rhythmic mechanical grindings assaulted her ears, but they slowed and faded. Strident, agitated whistles and clicks of orcas filled the resulting silence. When her boots tumbled into the unseen depths of the dark waters, Ace kicked to the surface.

Her head broke the surface. She cast about, finding her direction. The rust-streaked gray metal of the warship loomed on one side. Fog hid the ghost liner. She swept her gaze aft. The *Violet* rode on an even keel. If the hull had been breached by the collision, the leak must be slow. She spotted ropes trailing up to the warship railing. On deck, a dark oval of a face with wide eyes stared. She waved, then signaled thumbs-up.

As shots rang out, she motioned Sam toward the warship.

He waved back and began to clamber aboard.

Ace commenced a crawl-stroke toward the *Violet*. But a wavelike upheaval of water arose, scant feet ahead. Her heart clenched.

The hill of water rose. She backpedaled. An open triangle of a mouth erupted from the sea-hill. Gleaming teeth lined the gaping maw, easily large enough to bite Ace Carroway in two.

CHAPTER 29

In the boiler room, the engineer slammed several levers to their off positions. The roar of flaming fuel oil died, uncovering quieter steamy hisses and metallic bangs. Grumbling, the engineer and the rifleman jogged forward and climbed steep metal stairs.

From behind hot pipes, Quack poked his head out. He spotted only machinery. Not a swamp man in sight.

He darted over to a tool cabinet and yanked the doors open. His eyes roved. "Hammer, good. Chisel, yes. Oh, a file! Two files."

His arms cradling stolen tools, he scuttled crabwise back to the door to the hold. As he spun open the wheels of the locks, he watched for visitors.

But no humans entered the domain of the machines, and soon Quack slipped away as well. Shackles held Bert and the Hapennys. But, Quack vowed, they would not stay chained for long.

Tombstone cracked a shot now and then, forward up the starboard side, before ducking back. Gooper tossed grenades with decreasing frequency as his belt emptied.

"In poker, we call this a draw." Tombstone ejected a shell and slid a new one into place.

"I don't see 'em anymore, guv. They've gone to the trenches, waiting for us."

"How many bogeys you got over there?"

"Zero. Used to be two, plus the one that went overboard."

"I saw three at once, before."

"Where are they?"

"It's too quiet."

They peered around the corners of the smokestack housing, Tombstone to starboard, Gooper to port. No bullets whizzed.

They pulled back and squinted at each other.

A voice from astern piped, "Above you, sahibs!"

Sam stood at the back rail. Legs wide and arm extended, he sighted along his hammerless semiautomatic pistol. His manner so impressed the four soldiers creeping over the smokestack housing that one cried, "*Springen!*[10]"

Sam's pistol spat and flashed. Tombstone's assessment of Sam's marksmanship was accurate, however. No bullet found any of the swamp men.

Four soldiers jumped.

Gooper and Tombstone heeded Sam's warning and dodged. The rain of boots pummeled the deck, not the duo. Gooper plopped a meaty hand on a soldier's shoulder to hold him steady, then punched mightily with the other fist. The fellow didn't even have time to shriek.

---

[10] Jump!

Tombstone swung the barrel of his rifle at the soldier nearest to him. The soldier was too late raising his own weapon to block it and suffered a steel rod to the skull.

Sam, his clip empty, hurried forward. He was in time to intercept a third soldier before the soldier's gun swung to the ready. With his preferred weapon, a fist, Sam struck high, dodged a thrust from the gun, and struck again.

The fourth soldier recovered his feet. As Gooper felled his first assailant, the soldier pointed his rifle at Gooper's chest and fired.

Gooper staggered back with a cry of anguish, clapping a hand to the site of the bullet's entry.

The soldier pivoted, next targeting Sam.

But Gooper lunged forward and caught the man by his collar. One mighty yank pulled the soldier over backward. His gun fired into the air. Gooper made sure it didn't fire again, ripping it away from the fellow. Sam arrived to administer a pair of lightning jabs to the prone soldier's face.

Breathing heavily, the three assessed each other, then all three stared at Gooper's chest. The gold gleam of Ace's chainmail sparkled in the ragged bullet hole, stained with liquid red.

Gooper said, not without strain, "No worries. Never escaped from a rugby game without a hemorrhage or two."

Hastily, they stripped the weapons from the downed soldiers. One rifle they tossed overboard, the rest they kept.

They ran forward by the starboard side, around another vacant machine gun turret. The warship prow became visible, and an astounding sight met their eyes. The ghost liner lay ahead, split amidships by the gray bow of the warship. Debris peppered the crumpled steel deck. The ghost liner itself seemed all but cut in two.

The trio slowed as they passed the final machine gun turret, gaping at the sight.

Too late, they sensed danger.

Behind the turret lurked three uniformed soldiers. With feral grins, they aimed their raised rifles at the three associates.

CHAPTER 30

Nearness to death brings details to vivid focus.

The three Ottomans, their bitter faces steeled to kill, zeroed in on their targets. One had a recent cut on his cheek, dripping crimson. One wore a kerchief around his neck. One bore an old scar that bisected an eyebrow. Their authentic military uniforms hugged them like faded second skins. Their rifles foreshortened into black dots with squinting eyes perched atop.

But behind them rose what resembled a glistening black and white mountain, streaming water. Spray from its watery eruption spattered the soldiers from behind. Startled expressions appeared on their faces. They began to pivot.

Their mouths fell open in horror. The orca behind them twisted as it rose. A black side fin rotated into view, blade shaped and massive. Casually, it swatted the soldiers with unstoppable momentum. They bounced and spun from the impact. Two tumbled off the warship altogether, wailing as they fell. The third ricocheted to wedge between gun turret and rail, cruelly bruised.

The orca began to fall, too. As it corkscrewed back into the ocean, a black sliver of its nose split off and fell toward the deck. On second glance, this extra bit was a black flight suit with a wide belt. On third glance, it was Ace Carroway falling from the sky.

She landed barefoot on the deck in a crouch position, arms wide for balance. The orca disappeared. Wordlessly, she spun toward the remaining soldier and sunk fingers into his neck.

As the soldier writhed on his journey to unconsciousness, Ace eyed Gooper, Tombstone, and Sam. She couldn't stop a saucy grin from spreading across her face. "Fellas, you look like you've seen a ghost."

Only Sam managed to close jaws that had dropped open. "Memsahib! You have saved us!"

The orca poked his nose out of the water and jetted spray from his blowhole. Ace waved and called, "Thanks, Berlin! Now, go on. Goodbye." Judging that her swamp man would stay out for a while, she let him drop to the deck in a heap. "Any sign of Quack?"

"No, Lady Ace." Sam crept to the edge of the warship to check for orcas.

Ace's eyes darted around the steel superstructure of the warship. "Is the deck secure?"

Tombstone whipped around to scan the forward parts of the ship. The bridge, the huge gun and its housing, and the prow all seemed devoid of swamp men. "Not necessarily, ma'am."

Cries for help in German floated up from the water, but the associates took no heed except Gooper. "Standard-issue Ottoman ammunition," he said, "can't stand bein' dunked in dihydrogen oxide."

Tombstone scowled at the red-haired biologist. "Don't think I don't know what you said, blubber butt."

"Let's clear this deck," Ace said as she claimed her victim's rifle as her own.

Cautiously, they skirted under the barrel of the main cannon, searching for living targets. Ace caressed its silvery sheen with her fingertips. After she passed it, she glanced at it again. Briefly, a melodic trill sounded.

Gooper blurted, "Wot? Wot, Ace?"

Ace shook her head. "Not important. Tell you later. Careful. Bullets could fly any second."

When they rounded to the port side, they saw soldier shapes. Hearts in their throats, the Carroway party raised their weapons. But the uniformed men disappeared into the superstructure of the warship and then closed a thick steel door behind them.

Ace led the charge to the steel door, leaving wet barefoot water splashes on the way. By the time they arrived, the door was dogged tight.

"Solid steel, Gooper," Tombstone said. "I don't care how big your muscles are, you won't beat your way in there. Not this century."

Ace whipped her head around toward the wreck of the ghost liner. A metallic, drawn-out creak moaned like a sorrowful giant.

"Oskar." Her brows knit together. "Maybe he's in there, still. What a heroic sacrifice for him to make!" She addressed the men. "Gooper. Tombstone. See if you can find a way belowdecks. Watch yourselves. Sam, come with me. The ghost liner is taking on water. We'd better hurry. Something could break loose any second."

Because of the yacht draped over its bow, the deck sloped downhill. Ace and Sam ran down that gentle incline to the broken luxury yacht. Ace leapt across a gap of air to the forward half of the ghost liner while Sam hunted for a less perilous path.

Tombstone and Gooper turned away from the bow and began hunting for ingress to the ship. They ascended a metal ladder to the bridge and poked their heads up timidly. The bridge lay open to the air on the sides, silent and empty as the rest of the deck. The pair completed their ascent and investigated the steel wheelhouse.

"No hatches down," Gooper reported. "No doors at all."

"Durn," Tombstone replied. As he turned to go, his eye caught sight of a nautical map laid out by the compass. Red ink circled a spot, and he leaned to examine it more closely. "Seattle's marked," he said. "And a note. It says '10,000,' and there's a skull an' crossbones."

Gooper shoved his head between Tombstone and the map. He huffed through his red whiskers, "Death. Blimey! Roll it up an' show Ace."

Tombstone tucked the map under his lean arm. As they clattered down the ladder from the bridge, the moaning scrape sounded again. This time, it crescendoed to an ear-splitting climax. Forward, past the giant gun, the two halves of the ghost liner dropped away from the warship. The men clung to the ladder as the warship pitched backward strongly, then wallowed back and forth on its way to finding an even keel.

"Ace!" Gooper cried.

"Sam!" Tombstone added.

They clattered down the rest of the ladder and jumped the last few steps to the deck. Tripping over themselves in haste, they rounded the big gun housing.

They gusted simultaneous sighs of relief. Ace and Sam picked their cautious way from the crinkled warship prow. Ace carried one-legged Oskar in her arms. His head wobbled and his eyes roved, dazed. Sam carried a radio.

Tombstone and Gooper ran to meet them. The last visible parts of the ghost liner sank beneath the waves.[11]

The warship's engines throbbed and rumbled. As if shrugging off the momentary interruption, the massive metal ship resumed its journey. At its stern, ropes snapped. The *Violet* rocked, then stilled, becalmed in the nameless channel.

Ace settled a dazed Oskar by the big gun. "Sam. Tombstone. Call *Sky Arrow One.* They can descend and tether to the warship. Oskar's all right. We'll see if we can manage to get him on board the airship."

Gooper said, "Tombstone found a map. It says ten thousand dead on it wif a circle around Seattle."

Ace glanced at the moon crossing the meridian to the south. The warship's bow veered to port, and the shiny barrel of the big gun swept past the moon. The throbbing of the engines deepened. The stream of air that chilled their faces became windier.

"Seattle," she mused. "On a ship built to fire cans of poison gas. That's horrible. And desperate."

"Surely, the Navy would stop them," Sam said.

"After a while, yes. But the war's long over. They're not expecting an attack."

"And it's foggy," Gooper said.

"They've sped up." Ace's brow wrinkled.

Sam said, "They plan to go to Seattle and kill its citizens? Before being sunk by the Navy? It sounds improbable."

---

[11] High above them, Gallows clutched his hair and wailed, "Begorrah!"

Ace said, "They are backed into a corner. They no doubt think the worst of the Allies, so they probably assume they'll be executed if they are caught. Their choice is death sooner against death later."

The engines grew even louder. Red sparks flew from the smokestacks. The wind from the bow blew briskly.

Gooper said confidently, "We'll stop 'em. It's a day or two journey to Seattle. We can use the radio to call the Navy."

Ace said, "But we've tipped our hand. They know we are here. They are sealed away behind steel plating. They can steer by compass at least, and probably peepholes and periscopes, too. But they know we are here."

Sam said, "They grow even more desperate, then."

Ace said, "They will pick a target that is nearer."

"Wot, Victoria?"

Ace's head snapped up, and she scanned for the moon again. It now floated serenely over the stern of the ship.

"We're heading north," she said. "Oh, no. Juneau."

"Juneau?" Gooper said. "Crikey! At this speed, we'll be there in, what, two hours?"

"Less. One hour and change."

"Cor."

Shreds of fog raced by them as they stared at each other.

Muscles along Ace's jaw rippled. "We've got to stop this ship."

Chapter 31

Despite the chill of the vast hold, sweat dripped from Quack's brow. His arm muscles burned as he endlessly rasped the file across the stubborn loop of iron.

At long last, it yielded. A few taps with the hammer freed Bert from the ankle iron.

"Thanks, friend," Bert said.

"Glad you're free." Quack wiped his forehead in the crook of his elbow.

"All these barrels say 'giftgas,'" Abel observed from nearby.

"It's some foreign language, hun," Bette said.

"Don't touch 'em," Quack advised. "Ace was talking about poison gas before. These kegs might be full of the stuff. Come on, let's get out of here before they lock us in."

But they were too late. The door to the boiler room stood sealed, immovable, and locked. Abel pounded fists uselessly on the metal. Quack's narrowed eyes traced a ring of black around the jamb, an airtight rubber seal. The observation made his stomach contract into a cold knot.

A half hour after arriving on deck, Ace clicked a

sparker. Her acetylene torch fired to life. She flipped a visor of smoked glass down over her eyes and applied the focused flame to the edge of a massive air intake grille. She was dry, clad in a brown flight suit with boots.

Gallows hovered at her elbow. "Lucky you had a cutting torch in your airship, Miss Carroway."

"Welding is a special joy of mine, actually. Satisfying, peaceful, creative."

"I doubt it not." Gallows slouched against the intake and peered into the forward fog patches. "How is it they can steer with not a soul in the bridge?"

"Many warships have a secondary bridge in case the first one is destroyed."

"Aye. But how can they see?"

"For vision, no doubt they have peepholes or periscopes. I'm worried about them sniping at us through such holes, now that you mention it."

"You mentioned it, not I."

"True!" Ace grinned for a moment.

Gallows glanced up at the tethered *Sky Arrow One*. It stretched almost as long as the warship but much more slender. Moonlight outlined it in luminous silver. Shreds of fog drifted by, injecting wildness into the night. He returned to studying Ace.

Her concentrating face and vivid scars were lit by the flame and sparks of her industry. The sailors and soldiers inside the steel hull needed air to breathe, she had reasoned. Also, the fuel oil needed fresh air for combustion. Ergo, a ventilation system. And a way in easier than burrowing through inches-thick hull plating.

Patiently, she guided her flame through several

bolts, effortlessly parting them.

"You'll let me come, won't you? I'll be good. I'll be better than good. I'll be positively heroic."

Ace dialed the flame down and flipped her visor up to stare at the sandy-haired Irishman. "Not that I doubt you, Gallows, but why? Quack and Bert are nearly strangers to you. Stay in *Sky Arrow One*, and you'll survive this. Come with us, and I can't guarantee a thing." She resumed work.

"I've had a change of heart, that's all. A new appreciation for my fellow sojourners on this sad planet. An expanded vision of the duty of a man in the world."

"Why is it that I can barely force myself to believe you?" Ace said as she burned through the metal.

"I deserve that. But now I'm trying to make amends, don't you see? My thievery was bad enough, but my allowin' Mr. Langley to take the lawyer was truly terrible. I'm tryin' to dig myself out of a deep hole."

Brown's voice, not far off, said, "Trying to impress Miss Carroway, I'd say. But that's no reason to doubt his sincerity."

Gallows spoke over his shoulder. "That is very insulting, Mr. Brown. I'm not so petty a man as that."

"In the interests of time, I'll simply say: As you say, Gallows. As you say."

With one bolt to go, Ace shut off her cutting torch. She inserted the flat end of her sparker between grille and housing and struck it with the heel of her hand. The grille popped free. Ace gripped it. Shoulder muscles bunching, she twisted. The grille swiveled and opened a dark maw leading to the depths of the warship.

She spared a brief glance toward the Irish rogue. "All right, Gallows. Come along."

Gallows said, "Oh, yes! I'm in!"

Ace straightened up and scanned the ragtag group. Oskar remained in the airship with Vivian and Gilbert. Tillamook had joined them, along with Brown and, now, Gallows. With Bert and Quack still missing, only Sam, Tombstone, and Gooper remained of her associates. But she knew they hungered for still more perilous action.

A fearsome raiding party, it was not. But the ragtag group had gotten this far. Ace said, "Brown, take one of the German rifles and give Gallows your dart gun. Everyone, queue up. I'll go first with some tools. At the very least, there will be another grille to get through. Wait for my signal."

Before they could answer, Ace vaulted into the darkness of the rectangular air duct.

Seconds later, a metallic crash rattled up from the vent. Gallows visibly jumped. A scream, male, rose from the depths but cut off a second later.

Gallows tried to climb into the vent, but Gooper laid a hand on his knitted sweater and pulled him back. From down the shaft, Ace's voice echoed.

"All clear!"

Gooper and Tombstone shouldered their way in first, fighting for position. They slid into the shaft and disappeared. The others followed, but after being buffeted, Gallows found himself at the rear.

Muttering under his breath, the Irishman levered himself into the duct and scooted down the curve until he started sliding. He spread his legs wide, scraping his boots on the sides of the duct to slow his descent. A yellow rectangle below him resolved into an open air vent and a room beyond.

Abruptly, the side walls disappeared. Flailing, Gallows suffered an ungraceful landing astride the open vent. He groaned, regrouped, and stuck his legs through. He dropped into a room redolent of grease and dust next to the sprawled form of an unconscious soldier. Frayed areas dotted the soldier's Great War vintage Ottoman uniform.

A mass of levers and a periscope occupied one corner of the metal room. Doors pierced the bulkheads forward, aft, and starboard. Ace examined the controls as the men milled around.

Tillamook explored forward. "Where does this door go?"

Ace replied, "No clue. The engine room must be under the stacks, but a second bridge could be almost anywhere on the ship."

Brown joined Tillamook and spun the wheel on the thick steel door. "It's something to try, so, shall we?" He pushed. The well-greased door opened noiselessly compared to the ceaseless grind of the engines that vibrated the length of the ship. Brown stepped through the door into gloom, and the rest of the crew followed. As they peered around, their puzzlement grew.

A geometrical array filled the forward room, covering whatever might have been walls. Rows and columns of finned cylinders packed the space from floor to high ceiling, hundreds in the visible layer alone.

"Blimey," Gooper said. "Rows an' rows an' rows."

"Shells?" Tombstone asked.

"A variety of shell," Ace said in grim tones.

"Finned gas canisters identical to those that killed the crew of the *Sir John Thompson*."

Brown said, his voice unsteady, "This is the loading room for the big gun. It's meant to fire *these*."

Sam said, "It can launch a gas attack from — how far a distance, sahib?"

Tombstone said, "It's a Texas-sized gun, Sam. Range is gonna be measured miles."

"Their plan was ten thousand in Seattle," Brown said. "One direct hit killed the crew of the *Sir John Thompson*. They could wipe out Juneau entirely."

"Not if we can stop them," Ace said. "Gooper, get out of the light. I want to see the firing mechanism."

Gooper stood aside from the door. In that moment, a bullet passed through his just-vacated location and pinged off the oval doorframe.

Gooper and Tombstone hit the floor, barrels of their borrowed guns sticking out the door. They fired back, enthusiastically wasteful of ammunition. Sam, Brown, and Tillamook added occasional bursts of their own. Shortly, there was an anguished scream from outside. A ceasefire fell.

"Nice job, fellas." Ace compared the size of her pocket wrench with the bolts keeping the big gun together. She sighed and pocketed the inadequate wrench.

Her eyes narrowed. "Where's Gallows?"

The men sent glances at each other and the surroundings.

"Blimey," Gooper said. "Now where's 'e gone?"

Chapter 32

Gallows spotted movement at the aft door. In the other direction, only the backs of the Carroway party were visible. He smirked and crept aft. Stealthily, he cracked the door. Greasy light down a corridor showed the receding back of an Ottoman soldier.

Gallows tiptoed after. He left the door open in case he needed an escape route.

The corridor split, and the soldier went right. Gallows arrived at the intersection in time to hear rapid back-and-forth conversation in staccato German.

Feeling exposed, he minced past the corridor to seek cover. He caught a glimpse of a lit room in which several uniformed soldiers gesticulated. Further aft, a row of cabin doors nestled along the corridor. Gallows pressed himself back into one.

Conversation ceased, and boots clattered in the corridor. Gallows leaned out to see the backs of soldiers going forward. "Three of them," he muttered to himself. "I don't speak German, but it's a safe bet they know the Allies are a-comin'."

He sensed another and pulled back into the cabin doorway. Boots clicked at a hasty gait, this time in his direction, but only one soldier.

Gallows held his breath.

The soldier crossed right in front of Gallows. For a moment, Gallows wondered if he had escaped notice, but the soldier's head snapped around. The unshaven soldier gripped a Luger pistol in one hand and a ring of keys in the other.

Gallows punched.

The soldier's head snapped back and clanged against the far bulkhead. Gallows waded in. His back-alley past aided him as he brutalized his opponent. A knee to the gut, an elbow to the jaw, and a shove, and the soldier collided with the metal of the corridor and dropped.

Gallows retrieved the keys. He tucked the Otto-man's Luger in his belt, for safekeeping since he already carried Brown's curare-dart gun. He ran astern, deeper into the ship. "Keys, Gallows," he panted. "Means prisoners. If you're lucky."

Moments later, the corridor dove down a metal staircase from which heat and an especially greasy smell wafted. "Engine room here, somewhere. Or galley." A metal side door beckoned on the inner side. Gallows tried its two-foot-long handle.

Locked.

He tried the keys. One of them fit.

Gallows pushed the long door handle down. With a sucking sound, rubber seals popped free. The door cracked open. Gloom filled the interior space.

He slipped inside and closed the metal door to block the outside light. The smell of dead grease clogged his nostrils. He groped around him. His hand touched smooth metal. His eyes adjusted to the dark until he could make out a cylinder, tall as he. Next to it, another, then another. Under his hand was a painted label. He bent close. "GIFTGAS," it said.

A paltry few electric bulbs showed a vast inner space: the entire middle of the ship. The massive gas canisters clustered inside cage-like metal racks. The racks, in turn, stacked like crates in a warehouse from floor to ceiling. More than a thousand tanks of poison gas, all told. Curls of electric wires festooned the tops of the orderly arrangement of stacked death.

Greasy dust caked much of the floor, but a path from the door had been trampled bare. Gallows crept along the beaten trail, muttering. "Now, if these cans lie empty, I'll eat my hat. That means they're full. Faith!"

The trail turned a corner among the racks of gas tanks, then another. After the next corner, the path broadened. Gallows squinted. Dull shackles and chains draped around the hardware of the racks.

He inched forward. A faint rustle above made him look up.

A man dove from the sky onto Gallows.

Boots slammed Gallows into the dirty metal floor. The bruises punched bolts of pain through his body, but he managed a roll to escape a kick from his assailant. He rolled to his back and raised Brown's pistol. He squinted into the dark hole of a gun barrel pointing back. He froze. His eyes drifted up to the owner of the steady firearm.

"You!" he accused.

"I," Quack answered back.

Gallows lowered Brown's dart gun.

Quack did likewise. "Ace sent you?"

"She let me tag along, at least. Help me up."

"Is she near?" Quack lent Gallows a hand.

Bert, Abel, and Bette oozed from between racks of barrels. All three more resembled piles of dirty rags than human beings.

Bert said hoarsely, "Is that Gallows? Jump on him

some more, Quack."

Gallows said, "I'm tryin' to make amends, Bert."

Bert said, "You got a door open?"

"Aye."

The ragged lawyer managed a half smile. "That makes a few amends right there. Let's go."

Gallows stuffed his revolver in his belt. "Aye, 'tis high time for a rescue. The door is yonder. Ace Carroway and her men are forward. They're trying to stop this ship."

"Took 'em long enough," Bette said, rubbing a bruised wrist.

Gallows retraced his steps. The others followed.

They rounded a corner into more light than there should have been. A soldier's silhouette blocked light spilling in from the hallway through a wide-open door. The soldier sensed them, his rifle barrel seeking like a pit viper homing in on a mouse.

Quack palmed his gun and fired over Gallows's shoulder. The sharp pop punched their ears.

The soldier stepped back a pace but didn't fall. Gallows rushed forward.

The wobbling soldier held his rifle at waist level. Its muzzle spat flame.

Gallows gave a choked cry. Half stumbling, half diving, Gallows tackled the swamp man at the knees. The soldier toppled over backward in the doorway hatch with Gallows on top.

His rifle spat one more time. From a distance, there was a metallic ricochet. And another. And, faint but distinct, the hiss of escaping gas.

Chills of dread vibrated the spines of them all. Wordlessly, they pelted for the open door. Gallows found his feet and scrambled out, just in time to avoid being trampled by Bette and Abel. Quack shoved Bert through the door. The downed soldier lay half in and half out of the poison gas hold. Quack hooked him by the armpits and dragged him free.

The instant Quack cleared the doorway, Gallows slammed the steel hatch shut and locked the lever in place. Blood stained his cabled wool sweater in a blotch over his ribs, but he grinned in triumph.

A burning in his eyes and nose and throat commenced, urgent and severe even over the pain from the wound in his ribs. Gallows hissed in anguish. He stumbled forward, one hand clapped to his eyes, one to his freely bleeding rib cage.

Bert gripped Gallows's right arm. "Gas! Run!"

Quack gripped Gallows's left arm. "Forward. Into the fresh air."

They hustled the stumbling, blinded man along the corridor. Quack said, "I hope that seal is tight. My eyes are burning now, too."

"Explains why they need door seals, I guess. They're Ottoman holdouts, did you know?" Bert croaked.

Bette and Abel stopped short at the prone body of the soldier felled by Gallows. Bette's voice trembled on the verge of hysteria. "This is a ship of death."

Gallows uncovered his eyes and blinked amid streaming tears. "Let go of me. I'm right enough. As for this fellow, he's not dead, unless I'm stronger than I think."

As if on cue, the soldier moaned and opened his eyes to glare up at them. A trail of blood trickled from nose to chin, and yellow stitching spelled "Farnum" below the collar of his shabby uniform.

"Conscious? No. Can't have that," Quack said. The blond man pointed his mercy gun at the soldier's lower leg and squeezed the trigger. The pop echoed in the metal companionway. "Farnum" convulsed and gripped his leg, then melted into a boneless puddle on the metal floor.

Chapter 33

The firefight worked its way astern from the big gun down the port side. Corner by corner, the allies won ground. Ace excelled at spotting ricochet angles to harry soldiers hidden around the steel corners. Tombstone obligingly splattered bullets where she pointed. Each victory added to their cache of weapons.

Ace bandaged each serious wound, friend or foe alike. Gooper collected another spray of bullet shards on his shoulder, and Brown caught fragments of a ricochet in his neck. Tillamook collected a laceration on her temple. A bullet nicked Tombstone on the lower calf. The Texan frothed with anger over it. Not the wound itself, but the damage to his tooled leather boots. They bound the wrists and ankles of three wounded soldiers.

They peered into a side room. It was a mess hall, empty. They filed past. But movement inside caught Tillamook's eye. She leapt backward and clotheslined Brown by throwing her arm around his neck. As they landed together in a heap, flying bullets harmlessly impacted the far wall.

Brown squeezed his eyes shut in pain; his neck already contained bits of bullet metal. When he opened his eyes, Tillamook filled his vision. "Don't die on me, Chack."

His face softened.

Her face softened, too, and then she buried it into his chest.

Gooper announced, "Obstruct your aural canals, ladies an' gentlemen. I 'ave one grenade left."

"He means plug yer ears," Tombstone translated.

After the tossed grenade stunned the pair of mess hall snipers, they wrapped them up as well. Finally, they arrived at a closed steel doorway. Its solid, blank face stared at them eyelessly. It used to have wheel-style lock mechanisms, but the wheels had been removed.

"Time!" Ace spat between clenched teeth. "They are winning the battle of the clock. I'll be back with the blowtorch."

She sprang away.

Gallows held his rib wound and led the way back, retracing his steps. The passage down which several soldiers had jabbered had vanished. Now, a solid gray sheet of metal barred the way.

Quack grabbed the door lever and tugged mightily, to no avail. "Locked."

"The Ottomans are in there." Gallows gestured with a blood-slathered hand.

"Try your keys, Gallows." Bert squinted forward, then aft. "Where's Ace and company?"

"Keys?" Gallows patted his pockets. Nothing jingled.

"Lost," Bert said darkly.

"Where do we go?" Abel asked.

"I want out of here," Bette said.

Quack nudged Gallows. "How did you get in?"

Gallows scowled. "Forward, down an air intake. But hold on. We have to stop this ship before it reaches Juneau."

"Why?" Quack asked.

"They're going to gas it. Everyone and everything. Now that their scheme is found out, they've gone suicidal."

Everyone stared at Gallows. Bert said, "It fits. They're zealots, each and every one. Every time they spoke, it was the Glory of the Empire this and the Glory of the Empire that."

Gallows said, "Come on. Let's get you former prisoners up on deck, anyway. There must be hatches."

They scuttled forward as the ship vibrated and roared, hurtling headlong through the inside passage.

As they entered the corner room, a head with tousled golden hair popped down from the ceiling.

"Quack! Bert!" Ace said. In a trice, she reversed herself and dropped to the floor, along with a tank of acetylene, blowtorch, and hose.

"Nary a hello for piteous, injured me?" Gallows quavered.

"Hello, Gallows. You're bleeding." Ace sounded impressed. She tipped her head to the couple. "And you must be Abel and Bette Hapenny."

"Pleasure," Bette said faintly.

Ace glanced at Quack. "We need your impersonation skills. Get that soldier's hat and wear it. The name on his uniform is Baumann."

"You're a sight for sore eyes, Ace," Bert rasped.

The golden flyer gripped his arm and peered into his face. "You all right?"

He nodded. After a second, Ace nodded back and released him.

Quack removed the cap from the soldier on the floor and settled it on his head. "We're both blond."

Ace pushed a rifle into his hands. She said, rapid-fire, "Through that forward door is where the big gun is loaded and fired. Two soldiers rushed up and locked themselves in there, a few minutes back. Pretend you're Baumann. Speak in German."

Quack said, "My German isn't exactly fluent."

"Do your best. 'Let me in' is 'lass mich rein.' Quack, don't shoot any canisters. If you do, *everyone will die.*"

The actor's brows furrowed, and he dipped a nod of understanding.

"Also, wait two minutes. I'll send Gooper and Tombstone to help storm their way in if you persuade the gunners to unlock the door." Ace swiveled to Gallows. "Is that a bullet graze?"

"Aye, that 'tis. Just a scratch."

"Want to attempt more heroics?"

The Irishman straightened. A rakish grin spread across his broad face. "Absolutely. I'm startin' to think I've found my calling. What's on your mind, fair colleen?"

"I'm not fair, I'm dark of complexion. But I want to boost you into the air ducts. Try to find a path forward to the gun-loading room. Barring that, find the electrical cables. If we found those, we could cut them."

"I'm your man," Gallows said gallantly, though his toothy smile might easily be mistaken for a pained grimace.

Quack offered Gallows a knife. "Here. A swamp man, uh, gave it to me."

Gallows slipped it into a belt loop. "Because you're such a handsome fellow, aye?"

Ace crouched and made a stirrup with her hands below the air vent. Gallows placed his boot in her hands, and she lifted him into the vent without strain.

Bette blinked at the gymnastics. "I don't think I can do that."

Ace watched Gallows disappear then flashed a quick grin at Bette. "No need. Follow me. The stairs up and out are on your right. Quack, stand by. Gooper and Tombstone will be back shortly."

Ace jogged off, carrying her blowtorch and acetylene tank. Abel and Bette trailed her down the dingy steel corridor.

Quack double-checked the name embroidered on the bound soldier's uniform. "Baumann."

CHAPTER 34

Quack examined Bert. "In the light, you look even worse. Are you all right, Bert?"

"I'm all right. I'm no good in a fight, though. I'm still weak."

"What did they do to you?"

"When I woke up, they threw me in a dark room with a chemical stench, and—" He broke off. "You won't believe what else."

Quack winced. "I heard. Seventy-five dead bodies, well-preserved."

"Correct. I only found out who I'd been sleeping with when they hauled me out of there. The boss, Watts Langley, wanted me to draft legal documents."

"What? What sort of documents?"

Bert grinned like a skeleton. "Ones to declare the Port Clam area out of bounds to everybody. And to enforce it, too."

"Did you do it?"

"More or less, yes. I tried to be Sam and insert secret codes that said 'help me' and so forth. I found out something."

"What's that?"

"I'm not Sam. I couldn't manage to invent a cipher or whatever he might have done. It didn't matter, anyway. Before I finished copying it, somebody poked the ant's nest. Panic ensued, and the swamp men abandoned their hideout. The Hapennys were thrown in with me. The Ottomans acted like zealots. They swore loud fealty to the Empire and chanted chants. Everybody but Langley is German, pretty sure."

Bert paused to cough, then gazed openly at Quack. "I knew it was you that poked their anthill, deep down. I could almost hear the rumble of the cavalry arriving. What friends you are. What friends." He reached to grip Quack's forearm.

"As if," Quack said past a lump in his throat, "you wouldn't do the same for us. What happened next?"

"The Germans packed up and swarmed aboard this ship. By then, we prisoners were an afterthought. They shackled us in the hold where you found us."

Quack raised a finger to his lips. "I hear footsteps." He unlimbered his rifle as metallic footsteps clattered louder. The sight of Gooper and Tombstone rumbling around the corner eased the tension.

"Quack!" Gooper's red mustache stretched into a happy curve.

"An' Bert," Tombstone said. "Bert, you look terrible. Like the prairie after a buffalo stampede."

Bert's lips twitched. "Nice to see you clods."

Quack said, "Ace said we should try to talk our way through the forward door."

Gooper shrugged his heavy shoulders. "You, not us. You an' your voice, guv. We'll be at your back when you say 'charge.'"

Tombstone regarded Quack. "Nice hat, by the way, blondie. Ah almost shot ya, ya looked so authentic."

Quack marched toward the door of the gun room. "Stay out of sight, everybody. There might be a peephole in the door."

Bert stifled a new cough. "Don't shoot metal canisters, Ace said. If you do, we all die."

Quack led, threading through a passageway to the forward door. When his followers had flanked the door, he rapped on it with his rifle barrel and barked, "Lass mich rein! Ich bin es, Baumann!"[12]

His voice was an octave higher than his usual rolling baritone, and the German accents rang true. The transformation of his voice made his friends look again, to make sure this German was still Quack.

Faintly, a query came through the door. "Baumann?"

"Ja! Lass mich rein!"

The door clanked and rattled.

The men tensed for action.

The door cracked open. Quack butted his shoulder to it, but it didn't budge.

"Du bist nicht Baumann!"[13] The barrel of a rifle poked through the door crack.

Quack dived to the metal floor and rolled. The rifle spat bullets that ricocheted wildly through the companionway.

The barrage lasted only a heartbeat or two. In a moment, the door slammed shut and locks engaged.

"Quack?" Bert said.

"I'm all right, I think. Bruised ego."

"Aw, shucks. It was a long shot, anyways. Mebbe Baumann went by a nickname. Bowwie, or somethin'."

Gooper helped Quack up off the floor. "Or perhaps he's got a bad lisp."

Quack grumbled, "Well, we scored zero, anyway.

---

[12] Let me in! It is I, Baumann!

[13] You are not Baumann!

Which way to Ace?"

Ace crouched low at the portside entrance to the secondary bridge and vaporized hinges. Acetylene light illuminated a visor of darkened glass and scarred skin underneath. Brown stood by expectantly. Sam had been sent to the deck to ensure the bound soldiers were still tied up.

Brown blurted, "Bert! You're all right!"

Bert, Quack, Gooper, and Tombstone joined Brown and Ace by the metal door. Bert said, "Hello, Brown. I'm still breathing. How'd you get roped into all this?"

"Er, long story."

Gooper said in mournful tones, "We couldn't break in, Ace. Sorry."

Muscles along Ace's jaw rippled. Tightly, she said, "So be it. The gun remains manned and operational. Any new injuries?"

Quack said, "No, by some miracle."

Footsteps clattered behind them. The crew raised their guns, but it was only Sam. His eyes showed their whites as he gasped, "Sahibs! Memsahibs! The large gun, it moves! And I see the lights of Juneau from the deck!"

"They will start their bombardment any moment." Brown reached a hand to the wall to steady himself.

The heavy throb of the engines lightened and grew faint.

"The ship. It slows! Oh, doom!" Sam cried.

Quiet fell. Ears strained for the concussion of the big gun. Only the sputtering hiss of Ace's blowtorch cut the silence.

Finally, Ace spoke. "I'm almost through. Sparks fly on the far side of the door, too. They know we're coming. How many to expect in there, I couldn't say."

"Hopefully, a plethora," Gooper said.

"Plethora?" Tombstone asked. "Is that some sort of South American snake?"

The door made a clunk sound in its frame. Ace extinguished her torch. "Plethora means a lot, and the hinges are cut. The lock is still engaged. We'll have to bend or break it, and the door may flop. Shoulders ready? Together, now."

"Let's swarm 'em," Gooper said.

The door was about three bodies wide. Gooper, Tombstone, and Ace backed up two paces and ran full tilt at the metal door. The human battering rams smashed into the steel. Grudgingly, the door bent into the room.

Ace slipped like an eel through the slender gap, leaving the others to try again.

Two rifle shots sounded, then a male cry of anguish. Gooper and Tombstone hit the door once more, and this time, it spun off into the room, completely free.

Ace stood in a wide stance over the body of a soldier. She held an Ottoman rifle at waist level, trained upon Watts Langley.

Langley stood by a wheel and all the instruments one would expect in the bridge of a ship. In one hand, he held a Luger pistol aimed unsteadily at Ace. In his other hand, he held some sort of clamp with trailing wires.

"Too late," he said. "You are too late. We approach Juneau now."

Ace said, "The game's over, Langley. Drop the gun. We won't kill you." The men behind her filtered in, guns trained on Langley.

"No closer!" Langley barked at them. He waved the hand carrying the odd electrical device. "You do not understand. This is a switch. It is called a dead man's switch. I squeeze it, see? I squeeze it all the time."

Ace said, keeping her eyes locked on Langley, "Stay back, fellas. Keep talking, Langley."

Langley trembled and stared. White spots of foam collected in the corners of his lips. Red veins crawled in his staring eyes. "If I relax, explosives in the hold detonate. Many pounds of powder. Hundreds of pounds."

Ace paled. "No!"

"Yes. The deck will shatter, and with it the contents of the hold."

"The gas."

"Easily enough to kill every human and animal in the town. It gives me no pleasure to do it, but the statement must be made."

Ace's bitter expression matched her slumped shoulders. "What do you want, Langley?"

CHAPTER 35

"Lay down your guns. All of you. Get off Franz. Back off." The crew watched Ace. She lowered her gun. They also lowered their guns.

Langley half turned to speak into a microphone, eyes swiveled to track Ace and her associates. "Fire! Fire!"

All the associates twitched. Langley waved his pistol at them. "Don't move!"

"This is insane, Langley." Ace's eyes watched the trail of wires leading, presumably, to detonators in the ship's hold. The hold packed full of pressurized poison.

"It is justice! The merest tithe of revenge for the heaps of atrocities committed by the Allies."

Ace's eyes roved to Tombstone, then to the dangling wires, then to Tombstone again. He didn't see. Expression tightening, she faced Langley. "Please give up. Please."

"The gun does not fire!" Langley wailed. Tears began to trail down his face. "Did you shoot them? My brave patriots?"

"Nay, guv. We couldn't break in." Gooper's mustache bristled out like a bottle brush.

"Liar!" Langley spat. "It is the end. I can't go on."

"No!" Ace said.

Langley raised the hand holding the switch dramatically. "Yes."

♠♠♠

Gallows knelt in the air duct and held his ribs, trying to clear his head against the waves of pain that seemed to steal his very breath away. "I' faith, I've no sense at all! What has gotten into me?"

He glanced up, toward the fresh air and the wide world and the hundred towns he hadn't yet been thrown out of. He looked down, into the steel bowels of the warship. He peered ahead, into the darkness.

He shut his eyes altogether for a moment. And then he crawled forward.

Air blew gently by him, only slightly greasy. Knees complaining, he followed it around a left corner. That way led to a right corner. He paused to hold his aching rib when he found a grate under his hands, electric light streaming through.

Weaving his head from side to side, he peeked. The main impression was of rows and rows of stacked artillery shells. But these had fins and all were marked "GIFTGAS." In one corner, gas masks and ear muffs hung on a rack. Two men took their ease on the casing of a massive machine that could only be the hind end of the huge gun. Around the necks of each, a gas mask hung at the ready. Carts for rolling the poison shells stood in a line, queued up for delivery into the firing chamber.

Gallows unlimbered his revolver and broke it open. Three of the chambers still contained curare darts. He clicked it shut and examined the grate.

Small screws held it. Not very sturdy but impossible to remove from within the duct. Gallows contemplated banging on it with the revolver. As a tool, it might function as a hammer, but it would make an awful racket.

A metallic tapping startled Gallows. A muffled voice rapped, "Lass mich rein! Ich bin es, Baumann!"

The effect on the two soldiers was electric. They leaped to their feet and laid hands on their rifles. They shared a sneer between them. One said, "Baumann?" and pointed the muzzle of his rifle at the door's edge. The other laid hands upon the latch and deliberately placed a booted foot a few inches back as a doorstop.

"Ja! Lass mich rein!" came the muffled reply. Gallows raised his revolver like a hammer about to whack a nail. The soldier below opened the door a crack. When the second soldier began firing, Gallows banged down. His timing was excellent. When the door slammed and locked again, the vent cover dangled by one twisted screw.

"Hast du einen getötet?"[14] asked the soldier who had swung the door.

The other shrugged. "Vielleicht."[15]

Unseen, an arm extended from the ceiling. A blue eye sighted along the revolver. The gun spoke twice.

The soldiers yelped and looked wildly around. One stared down at the feathers protruding from his chest. The other located the curls of smoke and the dangling vent and swatted his fellow. "Es!"

They raised their rifles. Gallows didn't see. He had

---

[14] Did you kill one?

[15] Maybe.

pulled back and squeezed his eyes shut.

His heart thudded ten times. Below, a rifle clattered to the metal floor. Gallows opened an eye. Eventually, he crept forward and peered down.

"Ah, they sleep like kittens after the cream." He stuffed the revolver in his belt. Attempting to ignore the twinges of pain in his side, he slid his feet down into the air, then dropped down into the room.

The impact made him cry out. Spots swam before his eyes. Stumbling, he claimed the two rifles of the insensate gunners. Panting, he scanned the room. One machine full of hoses gurgled and hummed. He jabbed a rifle at it and fired.

A splat of brown fluid erupted and kept spurting. Gallows backed away. The machine's noises became more labored.

Ponderous pistons, the gun's vertical supports, relaxed with a raspy hiss. The gun barrel sank. On deck, Sam's eyes widened, as did Gallows's, below.

Gallows backed up as the hydraulic fluid pooled on the floor. With a glance at the paralyzed gunners, he let himself out the door.

"I have an unsuspected talent for sabotage, I deem." Gallows arrived at the crossroads and endured an impotent glare from trussed-up Baumann. "Now, which way? Portside, I suppose."

The omnipresent vibration of the engines faded. Gallows limped his way astern, stepping over several bleeding Ottomans on his way. He heard voices ahead.

Around the last corner, a cutting torch and acetylene tank sat, and a steel door lay in ruin. Tense men stood with their backs to Gallows, their attention riveted forward.

Gallows crept forward, squinting.

Langley sweated, and his crazed eyes bulged out. He said, "Liar! It is the end. I can't go on."

"No!" Strain laced Ace's voice.

Langley raised a hand that trailed wires. "Yes."

With a smug, triumphant grin, Gallows pulled the revolver out of his belt and shot Langley.

CHAPTER 36

Ace's lifelong training had sharpened her reactions and honed her senses to extraordinary levels. The discipline of her Wing Chun breathing regimen channeled energy away from tension and fear into a calm, alert state. Regarding Langley, her hope was to sever the detonator wires with a bullet. She had failed to communicate her plan to Tombstone, the former Great War sharpshooter. Ace's marksmanship would have to suffice.

Just as the situation grew critical and Langley seemed about to release his dead man's switch, he raised his hand, causing the wires to dance crazily. To Ace's astonishment, the feather end of a dart appeared an inch left of center of Langley's chest. The revolver's bang jolted her ear milliseconds later, but she could not spare the time to look. She raised her Ottoman-issue rifle, but the motion seemed to take a lifetime.

Langley, hit by the dart, released both his pistol and the dead man's switch into the air, and his hands clapped to the spot of injury.

The switch emitted electric sparks, blue and distinct. The circuit was closed. Somewhere astern, Ace knew, sparks flew, hot and emphatic, starting the chain reaction that would end them all and the town of Juneau minutes later. The explosion would shatter the warship and its poisonous cargo, and the cloud of deadly gas would bloom wide over the landscape, killing everything that breathed.

A tenth of a second late might as well have been eternity compared to the speed of electricity. Eventually, Ace's sluggish rifle raised, and she sighted at the wriggling wires. Her finger squeezed the trigger.

The rifle bucked in her hands. The wires parted.

Time capriciously resumed its normal speed. The twin reports of revolver and rifle mingled with shouts and pandemonium as Brown and the associates dove forward. They tried to grab the deadly switch to squeeze it closed again. Brown had the advantage of position and managed to catch the device midair. The rest of the crew heaped atop him, except Quack and Bert.

Ace winced in anticipation of the titanic explosion to come.

Gallows frowned. "Well, don't everybody thank me at once now."

"You tool," Tillamook muttered.

Ace's eyes narrowed in suspicion. No shattering concussion arrived.

Langley sagged against the wheel. "No. No! What's wrong?"

Quack raised a finger in the air as Brown held the disconnected switch aloft in triumph.

Ace's eyes flew wide. "Quack?"

He spread his hands, one of which held a purloined rifle. "I had considerable free time when they locked me in the hold. I climbed up to see what all the wires were about."

"On my advice," Bert said smugly.

"True, you shyster. Anyway, I disconnected all the fuses."

Langley tried to swivel his head toward the microphone. "Fire!" he said piteously. "Fire! Ffff ..." He slumped to the floor.

The line of injured snaked through the airship's lounge. Brown, sporting bandages on his neck, sat holding hands with Tillamook. The Mountie mused, "When I tell the superintendent all you did, you'll probably get a job offer on the spot."

"I might consider it," she replied. "As long as I can stay in the forests and mountains."

"Really?" His face radiated a joyous sunburst.

A few chairs down from the pair, Quack worked on Gooper with a pair of tweezers while Tombstone waited his turn, mournfully stroking his holed boot. Bert, Sam, and Oskar relaxed on the remainder of the furniture. Abel and Bette Hapenny were absent. They had mixed with the swarm of curious fishermen and officials from Juneau. Mouths a-wag, their tall tale grew taller with each retelling.

Sky Arrow One was equipped with a compact surgery at the aft end of the lounge. Ace labored over Gallows as he lay prone on the surgeon's slab. After tying off the final suture, she slathered cream over his rib and wrapped linen around his torso. Gallows had no quip for the occasion; he was unconscious from a generous dose of ether.

"Ow!" Gooper scowled at Quack.

Quack waggled eyebrows at Gooper and let a sliver of metal drop from his tweezers into a glass jar. He glanced back at Ace. "All done? That took a while. Did he have a bullet in him?"

Ace drew some water in a basin and began washing up. "Yes. Lodged in his rib."

Gooper said, "Wot're you — ow, Quack, you're 'urtin' me! — Ace, wot're you going to, erm, *do* wif 'im?"

Ace snorted. "Do with him, indeed."

Tombstone drawled, "Ace. You didn't answer his question."

Ace inhaled deeply and exhaled long. "Fine. Well, I'm thinking that he and Oskar might make a good team. I was about to propose we drop him off at Oskar's harbor. They'll both be local celebrities after all this."

Oskar blinked.

Ace shot him a grin. "Things are looking up for you, Oskar. I wouldn't be surprised if you get a medal for your self-sacrifice."

"That would be strange. I will believe it when I see it. But it is true that with the swamp men gone, I have little to fear."

"Gallows can help you with your business. He's clever that way. All you have to do is let him dive at the site where your ghost ship sank."

Oskar scoffed. "There is no big treasure. Some silver bowls, perhaps. Forks and knives. Candlesticks."

"Let him find out for himself."

Oskar's eye corners crinkled. "Why not?"

Gooper interjected, "But 'e's sweet on you, Ace."

Ace replied immediately, "Too bad. I need to get that jet plane flying."

Tombstone drawled, "The jet? What about th' titanium?"

Ace's grin returned, wide and bright. "I stumbled on a supply. Or, more aptly, almost hit my head on it."

"Where?" Tombstone said.

"An' 'ow?" Gooper added.

"Indeed, memsahib," Sam said. "I stand amazed that you found spare time in this last day to research alternate mines and smelters."

Ace tilted her head back and laughed from the belly. "No, Sam. It's right here. The barrel of the warship's big gun is *made* of the stuff. Given that we just saved Juneau, I think the Territory of Alaska might let me have it. What use would they have for it?"

Tombstone's forehead furrowed. "Well, hitch me to a saddle and call me broke."

Reclining Bert waved a hand airily. "Is good luck still luck if it's skill? Ace spotted it because she knows about, um, unpronounceable metals."

Taking time out from drying her hands, Ace flicked Bert with the towel. "Regained enough strength to be cheeky, I see."

Bert winked. "It's Vivian's coffee. Perked me right up. Go get a cup, Ace."

Ace stepped forward and leaned on the back of the helmsman's chair, occupied at the moment by Gilbert. The dirigible idled, lighter than air, high above the becalmed Ottoman relic ship. Ace gazed out and down. The weft and warp of the inside passage shone in shades of pine and azure, dotted with stubborn shreds of fog. Sun sparkled on the waves, and lazy flocks of gulls cast thin shadows on tree and water alike.

She hummed in appreciation of the view. "Coffee's fine, but there's nothing like flying."

THE ALASKA DAILY EMPIRE

"ALL THE NEWS ALL THE TIME"

VOL. XX.   NO. 3076.   JUNEAU, ALASKA, THURSDAY, OCTOBER 26, 1922.   MEMBER OF ASSOCIATED PRESS.   PRICE TEN CENTS.

MYSTERY WARSHIP THREATENS JUNEAU

PULP PLANT IS OPERATING NOW AT FULL SPEED

Two Hundred Tons of Pulp Are Ready for Shipment at Speel River Plant.

Working three shifts, the pulp mill of the Alaska Pulp & Paper Company at Speel River turns out approximately 25 tons of moist pulp every day, according to R. W. P. Lake, who arrived here yesterday afternoon on a hurried business trip. Mr. Lake returned to Speel River today.

The plant is moving along smoothly to best suits as circum-

International Relations Dependent on Education

HONOLULU, Oct. 26.—The Pan-Pacific Commercial Congress attended by delegates of the countries bordering on the Pacific has opened here with an inspiring message from President Harding pledging his support toward its high ideals of peace, good will and mutual interest.

HONOLULU, T. H., Oct. 26.—Education provides the foundation for international relations.

CATASTROPHE APPROACHING

Foreign Adviser of British Gives Remedy for Averting World Trouble.

NEW YORK, Oct. 27.—Assistance to the poorer that all Europe's economic disease lies not in more gold through loans have us a doctor prescribing for a sick man patient in the slim means of recovery after a world upheaval.

INSISTS COCA COLA KING NAME ACCUSERS.

Girl Will Marry Man Who'll Pay Parents' Debts

LOS ANGELES, Oct. 26.—"I, the undersigned, offer to marry any American-born man of some honor and wealth who is willing to pay off my aged parents. I have asked the Los Angeles Examiner to publish this.

"BESSY BEST"

MYSTERY SHIP'S HOLD FULL OF POISON GAS

ACE CARROWAY SAVES JUNEAU

SHIP TO BE TOWED OUT TO SEA FOR SAKE OF SAFETY

JUNEAU, Oct. 26.—Yesterday morning, Juneau residents woke to find an Ottoman warship hovering overhead. By midday, a coherent story had emerged, and it's a whopper. The ship, an Aquila-class ironclad, displaces about 10,000 tons, and its hold is packed with barrels of compressed gas left over from Great War stockpiles. The Ottoman ship and its crew have been lurking near Port Clain since 1917.

During the night, the ship approached Juneau with intent to poison us all in our sleep. The deadly attack was thwarted by none other than Cecilia "Ace" Carroway, the famed pilot. The airship and crew also rescued from the clutches of the Ottomans local

EXCLUSIVE PHOTOGRAPH OF LENIN'S 'RIGHT HAND'

NOTES

I hope you enjoyed *Ace Carroway and the Ghost Liner*. The fictional 1920s setting departs slightly from historical fact. For example, Lark Haven. The actual town is Lock Haven, Pennsylvania. It occupies a flood plain whose geography is ideal for an airplane factory. Its rich aeronautical history started in 1937 with the opening of Piper Aircraft Corporation and continues today. With a change of two letters to emphasize the aeronautical metaphor, Lock Haven became Lark Haven, site of Carroway Aeronautics.

Artificial respiration of the sort that Ace applied to Gallows in the story was not in vogue in the 1920s. The Red Cross manuals of the time recommended the "prone pressure" method wherein the patient is rolled onto their stomach and the medic applies pressure to the lower ribs. Such a face-down position, however, is less dramatic, so I beg your indulgence in allowing me to place Ace in a position more awkward than strict adherence to history would dictate.

As for Ace, now that she is supplied with high temperature alloys she will work to perfect her jet engine. With it, she will hunt the most chilling of the Great War's ghosts: Darko Dor, the infamous instigator of gas warfare. Marooned in territory Dor controls, Ace is stripped of resources until she is powerless — except for a four-inch bolt that she chances upon. Can she leverage the humble lump of metal into victory? Find out in upcoming *Ace Carroway and the Blind Panic*.

ABOUT THE AUTHOR

Wyoming native Guy Worthey traded spurs and lassos for telescopes and computers when he decided on astrophysics for a day job. Whenever he temporarily escapes the gravitational pull of stars and galaxies, he writes fiction. He lives in Washington state with his violinist wife Diane. He likes cats and dogs and plays keyboards and bass guitar. His favorite food is called creamed eggs on toast, but once in a while, he heeds the siren song of chocolate.

ACKNOWLEDGMENTS

Especial thanks to ghost liner champions John Worthey, Sonya Bramwell, and Heather Hayden. Love and gratefulness to my family, especially Diane.

THE ADVENTURES OF ACE CARROWAY

Book 1
ACE CARROWAY AND THE GREAT WAR

Book 2
ACE CARROWAY AROUND THE WORLD

Book 3
ACE CARROWAY AND THE HANDSOME DEVIL

Book 4
ACE CARROWAY AND THE GROWLING DEATH

Book 5
ACE CARROWAY AND THE MIDNIGHT SCREAM

Book 6
ACE CARROWAY AND THE DEADLY VIOLIN

Book 7
ACE CARROWAY AND THE GHOST LINER

guyworthey.net